Lock Down Publications and Ca$h
Presents

TIPPIN THE SCALES 2

Live By The Gun, Die By The Gun

I0564755

Written By

Christopher "Diesel" Hornezes

First Edition 2025

Printed in the United States of America

Lock Down Publications
P.O. Box 944
Stockbridge, GA 30281
www.lockdownpublications.com

Like our page on Facebook: Lock Down Publications
www.facebook.com/lockdownpublications.ldp

Stay Connected with Us!

Text **LOCKDOWN** to 22828 to stay up-to-date with new releases, sneak peaks, contests and more…

Like our page on Facebook:
Lock Down Publications

Join Lock Down Publications/The New Era Reading Group

Visit our website:
www.lockdownpublications.com

Follow us on Instagram:
Lock Down Publications

Email Us: We want to hear from you!

CHAPTER 1
VICTOR

"*Oh shit!*" he shouted in panic, as he caught sight of the queen of the Valdez family winding her right arm up.

Before he could move, she hurled a can of pop at him. It bashed him right in the face, hard enough that it exploded, made his head snap back, and made his gun fly out of his hand.

CRACK! BINK! WHAM!

Evelyn caught him before he could fall to the floor with a fast 3-piece. She punched him up with such devastating force that Victor farted when she landed the third punch.

She and ChaCha got on him and started stomping and kicking Victor like they was on some gang-banging shit in the store.

Stuck in a frenzy, ChaCha felt someone grab her arm. Without even thinking, she yanked away then she punched the old Palestinian man in his nose hard, breaking his shit. He flew backwards and hit the floor, sleeping and bleeding from his nose.

"Oh shit………prima! That's the owner!" Evelyn panicked, having seen the old Middle Eastern man every time she came in for gas.

"Goddammit!" ChaCha cursed, looking at him.

"Hey! Hey! He's running!" someone yelled out.

Evelyn and ChaCha both turned and saw that Victor was no longer on the floor, but high tailing it towards the door.

Fuck, fuck, fuck, fuck, fuuuuuuuuuck! Fucking bitch! he cursed to himself as he ran out of the store to his Land Rover.

He hopped in, started the engine, and slammed it into drive, when from the store, the tall woman that he knew ran the Valdez family business exploded out of the store, running right for him.

He grabbed his Glock 9 and started firing at her.

BOC! BOC! BOC! BOC! BOC! BOC! BOC! BOC!

People screamed and took off running as Victor blew at her multiple times, but missed when the woman pulled some shit that he didn't think anyone would ever be brave enough to do, or skilled enough, while getting shot at.

She dove forward, tucked herself in like a ball, then sprung back up right at his door. She shot up fast and socked him right in his jaw, ringing his bell.

She punched him again and again and again.

"¡Mal parido! You"re dead bitch ass nigga!" she screamed an angrily.

***

CHACHA

She did him like a chick did her cheating man when *CHEATERS* caught him in the whip with his secret lover, beating his ass like a goon. She didn't give a damn about his gun. She was going to kill him. Period.

But then he mashed the gas. The engine roared, then the rear wheels started smoking as the Land Rover started burning rubber on the gas-soaked ground.

CRACK! CRACK! CRACK! CRACK! CRACK!

As the Land Rover shot forward, ChaCha got him five more times before the SUV swerved to the right and approached the street. She let go just before he jumped out onto Lewis, cutting off on-coming traffic, tearing out of there like a bat out of hell.

"Now what, mamabicho!" she yelled after it, running out to the middle of the street, still stuck in a frenzy of fury.

***

VICTOR

"Son of a bitch!" Victor shouted angrily, as his nose leaked, his jaw throbbed, and his head ached. "You're all dead! Dead! Deaaad!" he yelled.

He grabbed his phone and made a call.

Diablo answered right away. "Yeah?"

"Fuck the stash house! I want those Valdez bitches in the ground! *ASAP!*" he demanded, approaching Ridgeland Street, and making a right turn so hard that he almost flipped over.

"You sound pretty upset right now," Diablo chuckled. "Did something-"

"JUST GET IT FUCKING DONE, ASSHOLE!" Victor yelled, then ended the call, so livid that he could literally feel his own body heat radiating off himself.

***

CHACHA

"¡Pendeja! Get in your car and go!" ChaCha screamed at Evelyn, as she jumped up into her pearl-white 2005 Cadillac Escalade Ext pick-up, sitting high up on 28" chromed Forgiatos.

Evelyn obeyed ChaCha without debate, hopping into her BMW, then flooring it out of the gas station, shooting north on Lewis.

ChaCha was right behind her. She could hear the monstrous supercharged V8 engine roaring from under the Caddy truck's engine hood. She swerved around Evelyn's Alpina, then she mashed the gas to the floor, zooming past Evelyn.

Evelyn put the pedal to the pedal, using nearly all 600 horses the twin-turbo V8 under the hood of her Beemer had to keep up. Sighing to herself, Evelyn couldn't believe that she had just come face to face with the man that had been trying to kill her brothers and her, and didn't even know it.

Wait 'til I see that mamahuevo again... I'ma chop him up into pieces and bury him in different spots all over Illinois.

***

MICHELLE

Kneeled on all fours, ass-naked, hunched over her man, Michelle was sucking his dick so good that his toes curled in his sleep.

Javi groaned, waking up out of his sex-induced coma. His eyes opened as she took him all the way to the back of her throat, going balls deep.

"Shit!" he cursed, eyes opening all the way, then going wide as he focused in on her.

Michelle added one hand and started jerking his shaft while she sucked his cock. Javi groaned and cursed until she made him exploded in her mouth. She kept on milking him, sucking it all up out of him, then she put on a show for him, spitting all his jizz out onto his toned stomach, then slurping it all back up, and swallowing.

"Wow... that was *great*," Javi said, happy for the wake-up dome.

"Glad you liked it. Now it's time to get up so I can take your braids out and get you back together," she told him, sitting up on her knees, breasts bare and perky, his eyes focused on her erect nipples.

"But my hair doesn't need to be re-done. They ain't even messed up, bae."

"Nigga, they ain't fresh either, so get your booty up, Javier," she demanded, then grabbed his hand and yanked him up.

After she took his braids out, she picked out his hair, starting with the ends so she wouldn't rip hair out of the roots, like she was taught when she was a youngster. When she had all his hair picked up into a giant afro puff, she busted out laughing at him.

"The hell is so funny?" Javi asked, looking at her with a raised eyebrow.

"You! You look like a Dominican Colin Kaepernick!" she clowned, laughing so hard that her eyes filled up with tears.

Javi gave her *The People's Eyebrow*. "Callate, punk."

She laughed even harder at him.

Putting on a silk robe, she hurried to go feed Diamond and Demon. From the fridge, she got out to big raw bloody steaks and set them in their food bowls, then poured fresh water in the other ones. They both sat side by side, obediently waiting for her to give them the command.

Michelle looked at them. She stepped away, then said '¡*Cóme!*' to them.

Demon and Diamond rushed their bowls and tore into their meat, ripping the bloody slabs of meat up like they hadn't eaten in days.

Michelle smiled at her tiger-striped killers. She loved them like they were her children. She watched them for a second, then made her way back up to her man, so they could shower together.

In the shower, Javi couldn't resist getting him so more her while they were under the hot streams of water that poured down from the custom *rain-down* shower ceiling. Music played from the surround-sound speakers in the bathroom;

Usher's *Superstar* was on, serenading them. He fucked her brains out as he held her up against the wall. She came so hard that he had to hold her for a minute until she regained feeling in her legs. He busted his nut after she climaxed, planting his seed deep up inside her.

They washed and conditioned each other's hair, then washed each other's bodies before rinsing completely off and hopping out. Javi dried his lady off, rubbed her deodorant under her pits, then he rubbed lotion all over her body. He loved pampering her like the queen she was to him. Michelle did the same for him, treating him like the king he was to her.

Then she dropped down to her knees before him and got on to blow-job number three.

***

In their guest-bedroom-size California walk-in closet, with racks filled with everything from work clothes to expensive designer threads and kicks, plain jewelry, to iced out drip, and other accessories, Michelle put Javi in the chair to her makeup station. She turned the surround-speakers in the walk-in on so she could have some mood music while she did his hair. Dej Loaf's *Try Me* came on, putting her in mode.

She blow-dried his hair, greased his scalp, then with her rat-tail comb, she started whipping him up. An hour later, she had eight zigzag cornrows in his head. She got out her Andis beard liners and trimmers, got his baby hair line and beard back looking like they were tattooed on. When she was done, she stood in front of him, with her mirror.

"*Daaaaayuuuum*, bae! You snapped, joe!" Javi said, looking at how crispy his lady just got him.

"I did good, right?" She climbed onto his lap and wrapped her arms around his neck.

He looked up into her eyes. "You most definitely did, beautiful."

"Good. Now let's get dressed so we can go."

"To where?', Javi asked, hoping she'd tell him this time.

"To where I'm taking you. Now get up!"

CHAPTER 2
JAVI

A half an hour later, Javi was dressed to impress in a dark blue Christian Dior track suit, with the designer's name monogrammed all over it in white letters. On his feet were white and dark blue Retro Air Jordan 4s. Around his neck were two long and thick white-gold Cuban link chains, both embedded with flawless diamonds. In his ears, flawless diamond studs, and on his wrist, he had pulled out his white-gold diamond-encrusted Richard Mille timepiece. Once he was dressed and dripping hard, he put on some Gucci Guilty cologne.

Sitting on the bed with Demon and Diamond lying next to him, waiting for Michelle to come out of the closet, Javi got a text from his brother.

Bro, I have a little situation on my hands. Not gonna' be able to make it to kick back with you tonight. Sorry, man.

Javi's face frowned up, then called his brother instead of texting back.

"What happened?" he asked, when Xavier picked up.

"*Maaaaan*," Xavier explained the crazy situation about Kenzie and her daughter, Neveah, to his bro.

Javi was shocked, not only because of his brother's selflessness, but because of how there really were some real losers that thought it was fine to beat women up.

"That shit is crazy, yo. Anything I can do to help?" Javi asked.

"Yeah. I wanna' find dude's bitchass so I can teach him a lesson," Xavier told him.

"I will tell the 1st lady as soon as she comes out of the walk-in."

"Good look. Bro, this shit got me *heated*. He really fucked her up, and not just physically. On *Tommy*, bro, I need to find that punk-bitch clown, joe. Me and Precious finna go *all the way* in on him."

"Enough said. Got a pic' or a name?" Javi asked him.

"Yup. Finna send it to you now."

"Aight. I will get back to you. If you need me for anything else, I don't give a fuck what time it is, bro, hit my line and I'm there, but... uh... do you think yo'... other ladies gon' be cool with a chick and her child at yo' tip?"

"I am a grown *single* man, 'mano," Xavier replied with a chuckle. 'Don't know chick own me; *I* own me, 'ya dig I'm sayin'?"

"Until Nena finds out," Javi laughed. "Love, bro."

"Yup. Love."

Minutes later, the door to the walk-in opened. Javi glanced over and went wide-eyed when he saw his woman come out, dressed in the sexiest tight red Yves Saint Laurent dress, with black sequined roses on it, embroidered with gold glitter. It had a low dipping cleavage line, long sleeves, and a mid-thigh length hem, with a slit up her left thigh that stopped at her hip. Her legs were encased in stylish black fishnet pantyhose with roses and star patterns woven into them. On her feet, she rocked white Saint Laurent stiletto pumps, with pointed toes and gold 6" heels.

Her hair was flat-ironed bone straight, parted on the side and pulled back, while the other side was teased forward slightly. Her edges were gelled down and styled with black gel. Her eyelids were dusted black and lined, eye lashes extended with mascara, lips painted with shiny hot red lipstick.

Gold hoop earrings were in her ears, a gold rope necklace around her neck, on her wrist was a gold Cartier Jaguar watch with the rings to go with it on her fingers.

Javi caught a whiff of her sweet perfume when she emerged. His mouth watered from the scent and the sight of her. Pantyhose had always been something that got his dick so hard when a thick gorgeous woman wore them, especially with a tight dress, or a short skirt.

"¡Diablos, bebe!" Javi shouted and jumped up from the bed, rushing over to her and swooping her up into his arms, kissing all over her face, dying for her to let him crack from the back with her dress up and a big hole in her fishnets.

"¡Javier, *yaaaa*!" Michelle whined while giggling at the same time as he picked her up and put her against the wall. "No tenemos tiempo pa' esto ahora, papi! We're gonna' be late!"

"So! Late for what?" he asked, feeling so sexually frustrated.

"Late for where we're going! Put me down, you damn cornball!"

"You bogus as hell! How you gon' wear that and not lemme' beat it up as soon as I see you in it?"

Michelle busted out laughing at him. "Aawww! Am I making your dick so hard that you're gonna exploded in your Tom Fords?"

"*Yes!*"

"Okay. I'll help. Number five, here we go!" she said, reaching for his pants, dropping down to her knees and taking them and his boxer briefs with her.

Javi looked down and watched her kiss and lick all over his dick again, before wrapping her shiny red lips around it. He cursed when she took him to the back of her throat, then he shrieked when she started humming.

13

She used a hand to stroke his shaft while she topped him up. In five minutes, she made him cum, swallowing it all with a smile.

"Feel better now?" she asked, getting up off her knees.

"*No!*" he frowned.

"Well, that's too bad. Later, when we get home, we can fuck all night, then all day. For now, we're out. Now let's move, crabby-ass birthday boy!"

***

STACKS

He cursed angrily as Kenzie's phone went straight to voicemail. He'd tried six times in a row, getting the same result each time.

He was *livid!*

"On the Fin, I finna *kill* that bitch, joe!" he snapped.

Magali lifted her head and smacked her lips. "You really gonna trip about a bitch while I'm sucking your dick, though?" she asked incredulously, on her knees in front of him, in the kitchen of the crib in North Chicago, that Stacks had just dropped a few dollars on to move in asap.

He looked down at her. "Bitch! Put this dick back in yo' mouth!" he demanded, then grabbed the back of her head and stuffed his dick into her mouth and down her throat. "And suck this muhfucka good! Suck this muhfucka until I buss' all in yo' face! Don't say *shit* 'til I cum!"

Loving when he got rough with her, Magali happy obliged him and let him fuck her face, stuffing all of himself down her throat, making her gag. She reached a hand up and cupped his balls, massaging them, adding to his pleasure.

"Yeah, bitch! Shit! Just like that!" he groaned, his head tilting up, eyes closing so he could focus on the feeling of her phenomenal oral skills, *wishing* it was Kenzie that was sucking his dick at that moment.

14

Magali gave him her best. The deep guttural groans that came from him made her pussy leak so much that it made the crotch of her red leggings look like she peed on herself.

"Fuck! I f-f-finna buss'! Oh *shhhhhhhhiiiiiiiit!*" he cursed, feeling his nut rising.

Seconds later, he pulled his cock out of her mouth and demanded she keep her mouth open. She stuck her tongue out and tried to catch every drop as he skeeted all over her face, painting it with his hot jizz. She moaned as hot droplets splattered her face. She closed her eyes and savored the taste of every drop that entered her mouth. She licked her lips of the cum that oozed down.

"Mmmmm, I love it so much when you cum on my face, papi, and when you treat me like I'm a whore," she purred to him, before grabbing his softening cock and kissing the tip of it.

"You *are* a whore, bitch." Stacks laughed. "You're *my* whore."

"Yes, I am. So don't be worrying about no other bitch, Stacks. *I'm* yo ride or die bitch."

Stacks pulled her up off the floor and stabilized her on her 5" heels. She reached down and pulled his boxer briefs and pants up, fixing him up like she was his maid. She then took him by the hand and led him into the living room, where the duffel bag full of cash that she'd brought sat on his new couch.

"There's $366,000 in all cash, bae," she told him, grabbing it, unzipping it and handing it to him.

Stacks saw all the bundles of cash inside. His eyes lit up with glee.

"Good job, lil' mama. We got a little more to pop off up this way, and my lil' lords is movin' 'erythang I gave to them down in the 'Raq."

Just then, a knock came at the door. Magali went to answer it, looking out of the peep hole first, while Stacks looked out of the large living room window. He saw Mikey's

Blazer there in his driveway, behind his sister's Chevy Equinox, which was behind his 300C SRT-8.

Magali opened the door and started snapping on her brother, as he entered the house, with wet hair, a dusty Nike jogging suit, and dirty Nike running shoes on his feet.

"Where the fuck you been at, Mikey? We been trying to call your ass for hours!" she told him.

"Joe!" Mikey squeaked, with an excited look on his face. "I was just at that gas station on Lewis and Glen Flora, in the Town, and shit just got to *poppin'* there!"

"Like what?', asked Stacks, somewhat interested to know what Mikey was talking about.

"These two bitches beat the *fuck* outta this dude, joe! *In* the store! There was a tall one that hit dude in the face with a pop can and fucked him up! His gun flew out his hand 'n shit! Joe, them bitches was finna *kill* his ass in the fuckin' aisle, but the owner interfered and got his ass punched in his shit! Then dude ran up outta the store, hopped in this old ass Land Rover. The tall chick ran out of the store, still on his ass! He started shootin' at her, but on 'erythang, joe! She *kept* runnin'! Her ass did some Navy-Seal-ass shit and got to beatin' his ass while he was tryna shoot at her! Fam, that bitch a muhfuckin' *G!* I ain't *never* seen no shit like that before!"

"This happened today?', Magali asked.

"Yeah, joe! I was there!" he said, hesitantly.

"Damn. Y'all got some real goons out here in *Fake* County, huh?" Stacks asked Magali.

"Fuck you mean 'y'all'? Nigga', *I'm* from Chicago. *Fuck* Waukegan and every town around it," she replied.

Stacks chuckled. "Aye, Mike-Mike, you pop that brick off, or did you snort it up?"

"Half for me, the other half, yeah, I been poppin' it off. But I need some D and some ice, joe! I know about a rave takin' place out in Zion, down in that duck-off area on Shiloh Boulevard."

One of your little gay raves, eh? Magali thought, giggling to herself.

"Oh yeah? Them raves be filled with dope heads, joe. On Ghost."

Stacks left sister and brother alone in the living room to go put Mikey a pack together.

Magali turned to him and spoke in hushed tones.

"You made Rambo suspicious of you, stupid!" she spat quietly.

"Fuck is you talking about, *stupid?*" he shot back at her.

"I'm talking about your little secret, you dumb man-slut! You know… the one where you think you're a *bitch!* Rambo told Stacks that you keep on staring at him! Rambo's gonna shoot you if he finds out you're a puñal! Stop doing that shit, Mikey!"

Mikey gasped. "Does Stacks know?"

"Neither of them *know* anything, but you're making them question you!"

"Question him about what?" Stacks asked, re-entering the living room, with a plastic shopping bag in his hand.

"His ability to function because he snorts so much cocaine," Magali said, thinking fast on her feet.

"Yeah, you do snort a lot, but as long as you don't start doin' shit that's gon' get you popped, and make us all hot, then you cool," Stacks said to Mikey, handing the young one the bag. "That's $5,500 dollars' worth of bagged up dope, and $2,500 worth of bagged up ice. You should be good with that, right?"

Mikey's eyes lit up like he had just entered Drug Utopia. "Yeah! Aight! Cool! I'm out, joe!" he said, then without wasting another second, he hurried out of the house and hopped back into his Blazer, dipping out of the driveway and disappearing.

Stacks and Magali looked out of the window, shaking their heads.

"Should I have just given him all that?" he asked her.

"Do you want an honest answer?" she asked him back.

"No. I just know, he better not get popped off with that shit, because yo' brother will tell; I know his type."

Magali sighed. "Stacks, if my brother was to get yanked and start snitching, *I* would bond him out and put one in his dome *myself*."

Stacks looked at her for a long minute, searching for any signs of bullshit in her eyes. She stared right back up into his, not blinking.

"I hear you, shortie," he told her, with a smirk on his face. "It's one thing to say it, but it's different when you actually have to put a muhfucka down, especially when that person is yo' own brother. Remember that."

Magali nodded her head, saying nothing else on the matter.

***

MICHELLE

"Thank you, tio," Michelle said to the man that had claimed her as his niece, since she killed his daughter's creep-ass murderer back in her early New York days. "I look forward to my next job."

"Ya tu sabe, little lady. Te hablo despues," Negro said to her, then the call ended.

Michelle looked at Javi, leaning against the fridge in their kitchen. "My uncle is going to put a trace on that bitch-made creep, then when he gets a location, he'll send it to me. "I'll have it by tomorrow."

Javi nodded. "Cool. Bro gon' be happy. Sounds like he really likes this girl."

"I'd say so. When is the last time you seen your brother bring *any* chick to his crib? Even Nena!"

"Never."

"Exactly. So, this will be a personal favor I do for him, and I want to meet this girl asap. For now, though, let's go."

"Where we goin'?" he tried again.

"To where we're going. Stop trying, because I am not telling you."

Javi sucked his teeth, then followed her out of their home, leaving their dogs with plenty of things to do to keep themselves entertained while they were gone.

Outside, Michelle and Javi stood next to each other, contemplating which car to take. Javi's Wraith was still parked at the front door of their mansion. Inside the garage, a row of unbelievably pricey automobiles sat gleaming under the custom lighting.

Michelle's exclusive ultra-bright *Designo Diamond White* 2015 Mercedes-Benz S65 AMG, a Brabus 700 edition sat in the 6th bay.

Under the hood was a *ridiculously* powerful BiTurbo V12 engine under the black engine hood, matching the with the panoramic roof, and the blacked-out 22" Brabus race-inspired rims it sat on that were wrapped in road-gripping Pirelli race tires. Its wide-body kit was one of a kind, the mocha leather interior was accented with blackened piano-wood wood trim. The multi-media technology inside of it made it as official as the business office of a Fortune 500 company owner with a Mercedes symbol on it. Javi had randomly surprised his woman with it after he'd had it filled with hundreds of red roses.

Next to her Benz was her 2013 Aston Martin DB9 Volante, sporting a paint job that the British manufacturer called *Morning Frost White*. The interior was rare violet leather and suede, matching the convertible top. The $320,000 V12-powered 2-door sat on factory rims.

Javi's 2010 Cadillac Escalade Ext pick-up was next to Michelle's DB9. He'd had it candy painted a *Root Beer* metallic color. The interior had gotten re-done and now boasted peanut butter alligator and stingray leather. In the rear was a pavement-pounding sound-system. The Vortech engine that the Escalade came off the lot with was pulled out and swapped with a supercharged and intercooled racing 6.2-liter V8 from a popular aftermarket company, then it was given a lift kit so it could sit up perfectly on the 30" chromed Forgiatos he had the rim company custom make for him, and him only.

Their eyes went to Javi's monster, which sat next to his Caddy-Lac truck.

The 1986 Chevy Monte Carlo SS was re-built from the frame up. Nothing was left stock. The suspension, drive train, engine, all hit up and made to be very durable for the obscene amount of power it had. The candy Royal Blue paint job flicked as if it had come from the factory in that color. The SS had the T-Top roof; the white leather interior had royal blue trimming and accents. The most noticeable feature the G-Body had, was the custom chrome 24" Chevy IRCO-style rims, wrapped in Pirellis.

The last vehicle was Javi's restored and did-up '72 Chevy Chevelle. It was painted the same color as the SS, with white and blue interior. Under the hood was a chromed-out 454 cubic-inch engine, and it rolled on 22" chromed Asanti rims, breathing fire out of the dual stainless-steel Magnaflow exhaust pipes whenever he stomped the gas pedal.

Javi asked, "Which-"

"SS," Michelle quickly answered, cutting him off before he could ask the full question.

"Okay. G-Body it be," he said.

"I'll drive," Michelle then insisted, and ran inside to get the key before he could.

Javi chuckled to himself as he watched his woman raise up the Lamborghini-style driver's door and start up the demonic-sounding LS7 Corvette crate engine. He could see his whip shake when the motor cranked over. He got goose bumps from the sheer sound of it.

She pulled out of the garage, stopping next to him, then she hopped out.

"Oh, I get chauffer services today, huh?" he asked with a chuckle.

"Somethin' like that," she said, then held up a blindfold.

"Maaaan, what the hell? Why do I have to get blindfolded?"

"Because I say so," she told him, then made him let her cover his eyes before she got him inside the passenger's seat.

Lowering his door back into place, Michelle went and hopped back in behind the Chevy's 3-Spoke GT Classic steering wheel, pushed the 'D' button on the computerized push-shifter pad in the center console, then started rolling.

She got to the end of the driveway and hit a right turn onto Wadsworth, then, looking over at her man, putting on his seatbelt, Michelle started grinning and mashed the gas pedal to the floor.

Javi flew back into his seat as Michelle unleashed 700 horsepower in an instant. The SS's front end raised as the crazy amount of torque rocketed them forward as if they'd been shot out of a cannon.

Gripping the wood grain steering wheel with one hand, Michelle pushed the SS like she stole it and hit a lick with it, and the cops were on her tail, all the way up to Wadsworth and Lewis Ave. When she reached the red light at the intersection, she came to a gentle stop. She looked over at her man and saw him damn near still imprinted in his seat.

She busted out laughing at him. "You okay over there, bae?"

He turned his head to the left, facing her. "You're crazy."

"Aww! Thank you!" she exclaimed before she leaned over and kissed his lips, then sat back in her seat as the light turned green and floored it again.

***

VICTOR

Victor groaned as his new temp secretary held an icepack to his swollen eye. His face was lumped up, and blood stained his expensive shirt and suit jacket. He looked like he'd gone a round with Mike Tyson and then went another with Floyd Mayweather.

He was beyond bewildered by what had happened earlier. He had seriously underestimated his opponent.

Inside the office of his Milwaukee terminal, Victor sat on a long leather couch, being pampered by the Mexican beauty. She had been attending to him like she was trained to be a maid. She was gorgeous, from what he could see about her.

Her brown skin was like coffee with cream and sugar. Her hair was long and a luscious brown color, reaching down to her lower back. She had a cute, rounded face, with high cheek bones, and slanted eyes. Standing at just 5'1" in her high heels, she was a tiny little thing, with a petite physique, and a nice round little ass.

Despite his embarrassment, Victor couldn't take his mind off putting his dick in her mouth, her pussy, and her ass. The tight-fitting skirt suit she had on, with pantyhose and her heels had his dick throbbing in his blood-stained trousers. She was so close to him that her perky little breasts were just inches away from his face.

"How does that feel, Mr. Gomez?" she asked him, just a knocking at the door came.

"Better," he replied, upset by the interruption.

Penelope went to go get the door. She unlocked it, then opened it. Victor looked up and saw who is was and immediately wanted her to shut the door and lock it back.

The plain-clothes detective stood 5'8" and was slightly overweight. The top of his head was bald, while the sides were gray. He had a thick mustache under a huge bumpy nose that looked like a brown pickle.

"Vic," the Mexican man said, with a sly grin on his face. "Looks like you got yourself in a little bit of a situation, eh?"

Victor looked at him. "Whatever do you speak of Barrera?" he asked sarcastically.

"Well, besides getting into a physical altercation with the queen of the Valdez family, and obviously, not doing too well," Detective Barrera teased. "You opened fire in a public place, in broad daylight, at a goddamned gas station that was filled with people."

"So, you're here to arrest me?" Victor asked him, as his secretary stood off to the side, quietly listening to the men talk.

"No. And I can't arrest Ms. Ximena Sandoval either," he told Victor, calling the Valdez queen by her whole government name. "You had a gun on you and attempted to start some shit with the young Valdez princess. She was defended by Ms. Sandoval, who just happened to pull up for gas, from what I saw on the camera that was outside the gas station."

"Then what the hell are you here for?" Victor snapped.

Barrera smiled. "Because, I just *had* to see the result of Ms. Sandoval's handiwork!" he said and busted out laughing at him. "It's all over the station! You got your ass handed to you!"

Penelope snickered to herself.

Victor ground his teeth in anger from the man teasing him. He started thinking about the .44 Magnum he had under the desk, with six bullets in it that would shut him the fuck up. But, killing the detective would not help, and Barrera wasn't just a cop to Victor.

"Now, if I tell your father about this, what do you think he'll do, huh?" Barrera asked him. "All those times I picked you up from school, because you got beat up by some kid, or a *girl*. You used to call me, crying your ass off; '*¡Tio! ¡Por favor! Come get me from school. Papa can't see me with a black eye!*'"

Victor indeed remembered the times he had to call his uncle to pick him up from school, so his asshole father wouldn't get to talking all that shit to him for losing a fight. What was pissing Victor off even more now, was the fact that his cop-ass uncle was clowning him in front of his new secretary, whom he hadn't even gotten to fuck yet.

He was making his *new* pussy think that *he* was a pussy!

"¡Tío!" Victor shouted angrily.

"Yes! That's how you would sound!" Barrera laughed even harder at his nephew.

"Con permiso, jefe," Penelope said, thinking it best she excused herself before Victor was embarrassed any further.

She scurried out of his office and closed the door.

Barrera got a hold of himself a minute later. He looked at his nephew and saw how salty he looked. Victor was about to speak when his uncle's phone rang.

Holding a hand up to halt Victor from speaking, Barrera answered his phone.

"Barrera."

Victor sat back and waited impatiently, as his uncle listened. He saw the man frown up a second later.

"Where are you now, officer?" Barrera asked, now looking at his nephew. "Okay. I'm en route. Take him to the station; I'll question him there."

Barrera ended the call then.

Looking at Victor, Barrera spoke. "Well, nephew, your mystery robbery may be a step closer to being solved."

Victor's eyebrows furrowed with puzzlement.

"What are you talking about, Barrera?" he asked.

"I'll let you know soon," the old man said, and made his way out of the office.

Penelope re-entered as the detective exited. She looked at her boss.

"Everything okay?" she asked him.

Victor looked at the sexy woman. He had to have her. Right now.

"No," he said, then undid his pants and stood up, pulling his hard dick out for her. "Not until I feel your lips wrapped around my cock. Come put it in your mouth, chula."

Penelope bit her bottom lip, then sauntered over to him with a look of mischief in her eyes. She went around his desk and stopped when she was inches away from him. Grabbing his hardness, she looked up into his eyes and smiled.

"Yes, sir. I would love to suck this cock, every day if you want me to," she told him, then she dropped down to her knees and let him stuff it in her mouth.

CHAPTER 3
KENZIE

The delicious aromas wafted into her nostrils, making her mouth water up as she held her sleeping daughter in her arms. She was laying on the big comfortable bed, in one of the plush guest bedrooms in Xavier's 4,200-sqaure-foot, 5-bedroom, 2-story house in Zion, right off Lorelei Drive. He lived minutes away from the Wal-Mart she worked at.

The big 85" 4K HDTV that was mounted on the wall across from the bed was on; MTV's popular show, '*Wild 'N Out*' was on the screen. Kenzie watched Justina Valentine murder DC Young Fly and Conceited in a rap battle. The sexy red head always killed whoever she went against, especially those that tried to make her out to be a slut.

Kenzie chuckled softly to herself, careful not to wake her little girl up. She still couldn't see what other people did that said she looked like the red-head white girl, but she considered a compliment, because the chick was bad a fuck!

A light tap on the door came just then. Kenzie laid her daughter down on the bed and went to open the door.

Xavier, dressed in a tight-fitting V-collar shirt, sweats, with Nikes on his feet, was at the door. With him, was Precious, his all-white female *Dogo Argentino*, of which Kenzie thought was a Pit Bull at first, due to how her ears were clipped like a Pit's.

Precious was a big girl for a 1-year-old. She stood tall at her shoulders and weighed 98 pounds. She was a *very* strong dog, and very protective of Xavier. Her lineage was comprised of many fierce protector canines, which included Bull Terrier, and the Cordoba Fighting dog. The Argentinean Mastiff breed was created by an Argentinean doctor to hunt big game, like Jaguars. A dog that could go toe to toe with a Jaguar… what would it do to a human?

Despite how protective and aggressive Precious could be, the second Xavier introduced her to Kenzie and Neveah, she turned into a big softie.

"Hey, Kenzie. I just wanted to let you know that if you and lil' mama wanted to eat, I cooked dinner; I made fried chicken, crinkle-cut French fries, sweet, creamed corn, and baked sweat potatoes."

She couldn't help but smile at him. She knew she'd be lying to herself if she was to say that the man wasn't outrageously handsome, and buff. Adding in that he cooked, and kept a clean house, even with how big it was, he seemed like a dream come true to her.

Kenzie was smitten with him, but she kept it to herself. Her daughter's well-being came first, and although she and Neveah were safe, she still wasn't on that with any man now. She was *in* the situation she was in because of a man.

She knew that very soon, she had to figure out a move for her and her daughter, because soon, just like many other single men, Kenzie knew that Xavier would grow tired of her presence. She just knew that a guy as handsome and put together like Xavier was, *had* to have multiple women. Kenzie didn't want to cramp his style.

"Um… yeah… we could eat," she said, still feeling so shy around him. "It actually smells pretty good, and Neveah hasn't eaten since earlier."

"Well, if you want, I could make y'all a couple of plates and bring 'em to y'all," Xavier offered, "or we could all eat in the living room, together. Maybe watch a movie?"

Kenzie sighed, leaning against the door frame. She looked at him, gazing up into his brown eyes, unable to help but get lost in them.

"Why are you really helping us, Xavier?" she asked him. "You don't know me. I could be a... freak or somethin'."

Xavier chuckled. "As beautiful as you are, ma, I would *not* mind it if you was a freak."

Kenzie started laughing at him.

"But on some real shit, it's just somethin' about you. I'm just... I don't know, ma. I feel somethin' for you."

She nodded her head in understanding; the feeling was mutual.

"Well. I guess we could all eat together. Neveah needs to wake up anyways, or she won't sleep through the night."

"Aight. You can go ahead and head down," Xavier told her. "I'll make the plates and set up the TV tray stands for us."

"Sounds good." Kenzie smiled at him again, matching his smile at her. "Thank you, Xavier. You're a very sweet man."

"I'll admit, this is a first for me, but I'm likin' how this is makin' me feel."

He headed off then. Precious walked up to her with her tail wagging. Kenzie patted her head, making the dog even happier.

"Hey, mama. How'd you get blessed with such a handsome papa, huh?" Kenzie asked her, stroking behind her ears now.

Precious grunted a reply, while looking up at her. The protectress was already a fan of Kenzie and Neveah, and, unbeknownst to the red-head beauty... so was Xavier.

***

MIKEY

40 minutes earlier

Mikey used the corner of his driver's license to snort up more of his cocaine. He took four quick bumps, two up each nostril, then he gave himself a gum-nummie. Throwing his head back, he snorted hard and cleared his nostrils. The sour backdrop then oozed down his throat, numbing it instantly.

His heartbeat fast as the cocaine sped him up. His breathing grew erratic; he was *fuuuucked* up and *loving* it!

Chilling in the parking lot of a Target in Waukegan, right on Lewis Ave and Yorkhouse Road, Mikey had pulled over to re-charged, before continuing towards Beloit, Wisconsin, where the rave taking place. But he wasn't Mikey, right now. He was in his *true* mode, now that he didn't have to see his sister, nor Stacks or Rambo for the rest of the evening.

He flipped down the overhead visor and checked himself out. His eyelids were dusted blue and lined with black. The mascara he'd applied extended his eyelashes out even more. Glossy red lipstick graced his lips, and hanging from his ears were chandelier–like earrings.

He was dressed in a sapphire-blue long-sleeved turtleneck mini-dress, with two balled-up socks tucked down in the breast area to make it look like he had titties. He had on black pantyhose and blue heels. He had flat ironed his hair and had it down.

At first, glance, maybe even second, third, and fourth, just looking at Mikey, one wouldn't be able to tell he was a guy, unless they looked at his throat and saw he had an Adam's apple. The turtleneck of his dress covered it, though.

"Ooooo! *Shit!*" Mikey shrieked as the coke lit him up. "Okay! Yeah! Time to get back rollin', joe!"

He started his engine and was about to put the Trailblazer into drive, when out of nowhere, a red STR-8 Dodge Magnum skidded to a stop in front of him.

Mikey's eyebrows furrowed up as he wondered what the hell was going on. Then, a second later, he saw who it was that was getting out of the car, and it *wasn't* Waukegan's famous *Jump-Out Boys*.

"Oh shit!" Mikey screamed when he saw Rambo hop out and point a Glock right at him.

***

RAMBO

BOC! BOC! BOC! BOC! BOC! BOC! BOC! BOC! BOC! BOC!

Rambo squeezed the trigger and popped relentlessly at Mikey as he mashed the gas and rammed the front right corner of his Magnum, pushing his way out of the parking spot.

Bullets flew into the windshield, but Mikey had ducked as he'd floored it. The Trailblazer swerved and had just missed hitting another car as Mikey made a break for the exit.

People screamed and ran at the sound of the gun shots. Rambo hurried and jumped back into his car and peeled off, having no intention of letting Mikey get away.

I knew that little bitch was homo! Wait 'til I catch him! Then I'ma put five of 'em in his thot-ass sister!" he thought to himself, as he rounded a corner of parked cars, catching sight of Mikey as he reached the exit to Lewis Avenue.

He banged a left at the exit, just as Mikey jumped out onto Lewis and hit a hard left, nearly causing an accident. Rambo swerved around the three vehicles that had almost slammed into Mikey's Trailblazer and turned left, flooring it. The supercharged Hemi engine under his hood had one more power than the punk-ass 6-cylinder engine under the hood of Mikey's SUV. Rambo gunned it, putting the pedal all the way to the floor, gripping his .40 caliber semi-auto tight in his hand.

But ahead, at the Lewis and Yorkhouse intersection, the light was red. Mikey swerved over into the on-coming lane to go around the cars paused in the northbound side waiting for green.

Rambo saw a semi-truck rolling up Yorkhouse. He saw Mikey's brake lights come on as he entered the intersection, trying to stop before it was too late. But it was too late. Mikey slammed into the truck's long trailer, peeling back the windshield and roof, all the way to the rear of the SUV.

Rambo slammed on his brakes and skidded to a stop. The semi, unable to stop on a dime, dragged Mikey's destroyed vehicle a few hundred feet, coming to a complete stop in front of a Taco Bell.

Coincidentally, two Waukegan Police Impalas were in the small restaurant's parking lot; the officers were inside, getting food as the accident occurred. Hearing it, they ran out, right to the crash.

Rambo cursed under his breath, praying that Mikey was dead. Stacks told him that he'd given the young dude a pack to move at the rave, and it was %100 for sure that it was all inside the Trailblazer.

Slamming it into reverse, Rambo hit the gas and shot backwards, whipping his steering wheel to the left, and spinning his Magnum to the right, then he slammed it into drive and mashed the gas. Taking off, he headed south, angry that he'd fucked up. Getting his phone out of his pocket, he immediately called Stacks, to deliver the news.

CHAPTER 4
JAVI

Javi couldn't see anything, no matter how many times he wiggled his nose to make the blind-fold shift, to give him just a peek.

Five minutes ago, he had felt Michelle pull into somewhere and stop, then a few seconds after, his door was opened, and he felt her take his hand and help him out. He asked where they were, just for fucks sake. She refused to tell him, giggling instead.

He could tell they went into a building, then into an elevator. Michelle was still holding his left arm, standing at his side as the elevator went up.

"Lemme' find out you're mad at me and 'bout to push me off the top of a building, man," he told her.

His head went to the right as she muffed him.

"Shut cha' ass up, Javier," he heard her say.

DING!

The sound of the bell told Javi that they'd reached whatever floor they were going to, which by how long the ride up was, he could tell they were very high.

"Ready, baby?" he heard his woman ask him.

"I been ready since you put this damn thing on me, Michelle," he replied grumpily.

She muffed his head again. "No seas un *mamao*, mamao."

Javi chuckled, just as he heard the doors open.

Michelle guided him forward, then she stopped him.

"Okay, birthday boy," she said, then counted down from three.

Once she reached zero, Michelle took the blind fold off.

"*Suuurrrppprriissee!*" a huge crowd of family and friends all yelled at the same time, shocking the ever-loving *shit* out of Javi. "*HAPPY BIRTHDAY, JAVIER!*"

"Whoa..." Javi expected a surprise b-day dinner, or maybe a few friends, but not this.

Michelle saw the look of sheer astonishment on her man's face and was elated. She and ChaCha had been planning the surprise b-day bash for Javi for a few months. Besides all sorts of gifts, and all the people, there were two things, one of which she had managed to put together on her own, that she knew Javi was going to go bananas over when he saw them.

In front of the crowd, Javi saw his caramel-skinned grandfather Diego, who was built like a 6'1" Ox, and his brown-sugar-complexioned grandmother Maritza.

With them was the fair-skinned Juanito, Javi's great uncle, and his lighter-brown-skinned great aunt Carolína. Javi was surprised to see that his eldest great aunt, Larissa, a gray-haired woman with butter pecan-brown skin and the looks of a woman 30 years her junior, there at the bash. Since Pedro passed, Larissa barely ever left the Dominican Republic, unless for a family special event, or to go see her son Danny, in prison.

ChaCha of course was there, dressed in a flowing pearl-colored Carolina Herrera one-shoulder dress that went all the way down past her knees, to her calves. T-strapped stiletto pumps were on her feet; her hair was pinned up like she was a ballroom dancer. Her diamond jewelry sparkled like cameras flashed a hundred times a second from inside each rock.

Standing with her was Tool, and another woman, that had a strong resemblance to ChaCha.

Javi then saw his baby sister and grew furious.

"¡¿Que carajo es eso?!" he asked, seeing Evelyn in a ridiculously tight and very short YSL bodice dress that were only worn in magazines.

It was made of silk, champagne-colored with gold tassels at the mid-thigh length hem. The top made her breasts look so much bigger. If she bent over, even just a little, or didn't cross her legs when she sat down, she would most definitely be on *full* display.

She looked like she would be posing for one of the popular Urban model magazines that littered the eye-candy market, with her long hair flat-iron and parted right up the middle of her head and let to hang loose down her shoulders. She was made up like a video vixen and iced out with diamond-encrusted jewelry. Down on her feet, Evelyn rocked diamond-studded YSL pumps.

Next to her, Gloria had on a chocolate-colored body suit that made it look like she was ass-naked, but Javi didn't give a damn about how *she* dressed.

"Bae, what's up?" asked Michelle, looking at her man's aggravated facial expression.

ChaCha, his sister, Gloria, Tool, and grandparents all wondered the same.

"Why in the hell is my baby sister dressed like that with our grandparents here?!" Javi demanded to know, glaring at Evelyn angrily as she smacked her lips and folded her arms over her bosom.

"I'm a grown woman, *that's* why!" Evelyn snapped back.

"Javier," Maritza said to him, stepping in front of her oldest grandson. "Tranquilo, cariño. Tu hermana pequeña es una mujer muy hermosa. She is proud of how she looks, so she shows it off."

"She doesn't gotta be dressed like a *thot* to do it, abuela!" Javi shot back, still so livid with Evelyn.

"Javier!" Michelle yelled, grabbing him by his shoulder. "¡Cuida la maldita boca ahora mismo! That's your baby sister!"

Evelyn's eyes started welling up with tears from her brother being so angry at her. Javi saw it and immediately felt like an asshole. He looked at his family and saw so many heads shaking in disdain at him.

He was about to apologize to her, when suddenly, the crowd parted, and he saw two people coming through that made him think he was seeing ghosts.

"No…way," he said, not believing his eyes. "*Ma? Pop?*" You're… *here*?"

Ricardo and Roselyn Valdez were indeed there, in the flesh. Ricardo, dark-skinned like his youngest son, had long braids like his oldest, and even had green eyes. He was 6'4, built like an athlete, and had a few tattoos on his arms. He was dressed in a pin-striped Armani suit, with the fedora to match. Cartier shades hid his eyes, and a Cartier watch was on his wrist. The diamond wedding ring on his finger was a fraction of what was on his wife's finger.

Roselyn was the older version of Evelyn. She was golden-brown with golden-blonde hair and was very voluptuous. She was even the same height as her daughter. Roselyn was the epitome of stunning. Neither she nor her husband looked a day over 25 years old. To learn that they were both in their early 40s made so many people think they'd discovered the fountain of youth somewhere.

Their current looks, however, were *pissed off*. Ricardo approached his oldest son with his wife next to him and took his shades off. He took his time, folding them in, then tucking them down into the breast pocket of his Armani suit jacket.

Javi swallowed hard. He hadn't seen his parents in years, but he remembered what it looked like when he was in trouble.

"Javier," Ricardo said, cool, calm, collected. "If I ever, hear you speak to your baby sister like that again." Ricardo looked his son in his eyes then. "You and I are gonna' have a big problem. ¿Me entiendes, mijo?"

Javi nodded his head. "Y-Yes, sir. I-I'm sorry, pop."

"¡Dile eso a ella!" Ricardo exploded.

Everyone watched as Javi went to his sister and begged her forgiveness.

"Maybe," she replied, snootily.

"¿De que hablas 'maybe', Eve?" he asked with a puzzled look.

"I want another truck," she told him, "and, I want my trailer painted to match my new one, and you know what? Gloria needs a new one, and so does Olivia, Kiara, Jada, and Payton."

Javi frowned up. "You forgot Nena," he told her, seeing his brother's honey-dip in the group of female drivers that worked for his sister's auto-transport division, of whom were all dolled up and dressed as scantily as their bosses.

"Nena doesn't get a new truck until she stops breaking the one that she has that is still freakin' *new* and hasn't even reached 10,000 miles yet!" Evelyn said, then shot a look over at Nena, making the Pilsen girl try hiding behind Olivia.

"Aight." Javi nodded his head. "You got it. Will you forgive me now, so ma stops grillin' me?" he asked, seeing how their mother was staring daggers into him. He started pleading with her, because respect was big in his family, and he knew he was wrong. "I am *sorry*, Eve. I only got mad because I know how motherffff," he paused before he cursed and ended up feeling an open hand across his face. "I know how these dudes think when it comes to women dressed in provocative ways. Guys be grown, 30s, 40s, 50s, and older, be tryna get at little young girls like you, like some straight up *creeps!*"

"I understand, bro," Evelyn said then. "I need you to remember that I can handle myself, and you've *seen* me handle myself. And there isn't a single woman in here that isn't looking super sexy. Look at mom!"

"No! *Hell* no! Are you drunk?! Why the hell would I look at our mother to see how sexy she is?! You tweakin'!"

Evelyn and the crowd burst out laughing at Javi. Roselyn went to her son and threw her arms around him, kissing his face.

"Feliz cumpleaños, papacito," she told him, hugging him tightly.

"Thank you, ma. Te extrañé mucho. Both of y'all."

"We' missed you three, too, papa," Ricardo said, patting his son's shoulder.

"Are y'all back for good now?" asked Evelyn, hoping to God they said yes so, they could all be together again.

"Soon, hija," Ricardo told her. "Very soon."

The two then greeted Michelle with emphatic hugs and kisses. They loved her like she was their daughter, and they couldn't wait for the day that their oldest son made her his wife.

Ricardo then asked where Xavier was, saddened at the fact that all three of his children were not present.

In a nutshell, Javi explained the situation to his mother and father.

"Ay, my kind-hearted gentle giant son," Roselyn said with a smile. "He was always a softie when it came to the mujeres."

"Pero un tiguere to the men that bothered him or his siblings," Ricardo added. "My sons are kings, and my daughter is a queen. I am a happy man for that."

Evelyn's crew stepped up then, to wish Javi a happy birthday. Olivia, formerly a tanker truck driver, was a 26-year-old Sicilian and Japanese-mixed chick that was 5'9 and petite, with an olive skin tone, and long black ass-length hair, from Joliet, hugged him and kissed him on his cheek.

Kiara and Jada, two 24-year-old ebony-skinned twin sisters that looked like clones of each other, were 5'6, thick as heel, with dreadlocks, spoke with southern twangs that had stuck with them, despite having moved from Birmingham, Alabama years ago, when they switched from driving semis for C.R.S.T Expedited.

Payton was a crazy thick Jamaican chick that was born in America. Her skin was as dark as a starless midnight skin. She stood 5'8" and was stacked like a brick house. She wore her hair in 2-strand twists, but they were not dreadlocked.

Then, there was Nena, the triple mutt with a fat butt, cute face, and high sex drive that broke trucks.

"Happy b-day, boss man" the twins said at the same time.

"Thanks, Ki-Ki and Jay," Javi replied, hugging them both as cameras flashed, capturing the three of them with smiles.

Olivia got a picture with Javi next, then wished him a happy birthday.

Payton bear-hugged him, then she punched him in his arm, 25 times.

"Goddammit, Payton!" Javi rubbed his arm. "Who you think you is?! Holly Holmes or Rhonda Rousey?! Strong-ass, man!"

Payton and the girls laughed at him, then they took Evelyn and scurried off to go get some drinks.

"Javi?"

He turned and saw Nena there, just as Xavier's two heavy-haul homies, Thurgood and Pete came to show their love, followed by Javi's crew.

Nena had on a green bob-style wig, red eye shadow, red lipstick, and a green skin-tight backless neck-strap dress, covered with cheetah spots. A long slit went up from the ankle-length hem, up to her left hip. Javi had to will himself to not look at his brother's dip like that, but that was almost impossible to do. Nena was *bad!*

"Yes, Nena?" Javi replied, as ChaCha, Tool, and the girl that was with ChaCha walked up to him.

"Is Xavier coming? He hasn't been answering any of my calls or texts, and I *really* need to tell him something."

"He's not gonna' make it, Nena. He had something he had to handle," Michelle told her.

She looked at Michelle. "Well… do you know where he is?"

"No. I'm sorry."

Nena looked back at Javi. He shrugged his shoulders. Nena then blew out an exasperated breath before taking her leave before anyone saw the tears welling up in her eyes.

"That girl is *gone* over bro, yo," Jav said to his lady.

"She is whooped in him," Michelle added.

"¡Oye, papito!" said ChaCha, wanting the vibe to come back to the light. "¡Dame hug, dame hug!" wrapping her arms around him and squeezing him. "Happy birthday, baby boy."

"Thanks, prima. Tool, what's good, big cuz?"

"You," the giant dread replied, then picked up a large black box that had been by his foot and handed it to Javi. "Happy birthday, lil' cutty."

"Grassy-ass, family," Javi replied goofily.

"Javier," ChaCha called to him, ushering the young woman she was with forward. "Do you remember this girl?"

Javi looked at the woman. She was very buxom, robust, voluptuous, a straight stallion by definition. She looked so much like ChaCha but had a more Middle Eastern-look to her.

Her raven-colored hair was long and luscious. Her face was just a little rounder than ChaCha's. Her body was so cold; Curvy and thick. She rocked a purple form-fitting, shoulderless, leather mini-dress, with purple ankle-strapped pumps on her feet that made her 5'11" figure looks so statuesque.

Javi studied her face for a second. She smiled, seeing him trying hard to place where he knew her from.

Then it hit him.

"*'Nessa!*" he shouted with wide eyes.

39

Vanessa chuckled and nodded. "Bingo. What took you so long, yo?" she asked him, in a voice so sweet and grown woman that it made Javi instantly realize that the little girl he remembered his little brother being so in love with when they were kids, was now a grown-ass woman.

Vanessa was ChaCha's younger cousin; their mothers were sisters. She was a half breed like her, but instead of her other half being Colombian, Vanessa's father was full-blooded Persian.

Javi remembered like it was yesterday, that the Puerto Rican-Persian beauty was his brother's heart back when they were all youngsters. They'd lived in Pittsburgh, Pennsylvania, with their older cousins Macho and Tool, for a couple of years, back when they were all learning how to drive trucks. Xavier had been stupid in love with her and so had she with him. ChaCha and Vanessa had both came to live in Pittsburgh from New York, which was where ChaCha initially met the head honcho of the Valdez family.

"Well, you *are* grown as hell now," Javi told her, stuck in disbelief that the girl in front of him was Vanessa Sandoval, whom when he had last seen her, she had no breasts, no hips, no ass, and was a tom boy.

"I think he's tryna say that he didn't remember you because you got thick as hell," ChaCha joked, then gave Vanessa's fat round leather-clad 46" ass a slap.

"Ow! Damnit, ChaCha! Leather!" Vanessa shouted, rubbing her stinging ass.

They all busted out laughing at Vanessa and ChaCha.

"Anyways, how you been, lil' cuzzo?" Javi asked Vanessa. "It's been *waaaay* too long since the last time I saw you; Xavier, too."

At the mention of his name, Vanessa started blushing.

They all saw her turning rosy red.

"Oooooo! Lemme' find out that 'Ness Neezy is *still* in love with Zay-Zay!" ChaCha clowned, calling them both by the nicknames they called each other when they were kids.

In his peripheral, Javi saw Nena's face scrunch up. He turned his head all the way and saw her crane her neck, likely trying to see who was said to still be in love with *her* man.

"ChaCha! Shut up, man! Damn! You're such an asshole!" Vanessa whined, completely embarrassed.

"Deja de llorar, big-booty-biatch," ChaCha laughed, hooking her arm around her little cousin's neck, just as Don Omar and Tego Calderon's *Bandaleros* started playing.

Javi chuckled at the two. He admired how close they were, and how they always bickered. It reminded him of how he was with his cousin Macho, and thinking about his cousin, being stuck in prison, instead of at the party with him and the family, lowered Javi's mood. He missed his cousin. They were close, and he hated the fact that Macho was there because he took a pistol case for a snake that absolutely *nobody* liked, nor respected, except for Macho for some reason.

"Aye, lil' cutty."

Javi heard a voice behind him that sounded *so* very familiar, but there was absolutely *no* way that it could belong to who it sounded like. He thought for a second that he was tweaking, but when he turned around, he discovered that he was not tweaking at all.

"¡Oye! ¡Primo! ¡Tiguerasooo!" shouted Javi when he saw his cousin Macho there, with his woman, and their best friend.

Inside, Michelle jumped for joy, overly excited that her second surprise had her man so hyped up. She knew Javi would be ecstatic to see *El Tiguere* in the house, free from prison.

The 6'3" braided-up goon was built like a heavy-weight boxer. He was 240 pounds of rock-hard muscle and gangster. His skin was golden-brown, just like Javi's, and he, too, had been blessed with colored eyes. His were bluish gray, like looking out a frosted window at an icy blue body of water.

Macho had arms the size of pythons, tattooed up, a barrel chest, shoulders like Zeus. His face, strong and model-like, with high cheekbones. His long hair was braided in neat intricate Iverson's, the long tails hung down to his wide chest, and his baby hair line and beard/goatee, lined up so sharp that they looked tattooed on.

Antonio Tomás Valdez, a.k.a *Macho*, was Javi's 25-year-old cousin, who looked more like he could big Javi's older brother. Macho was a member of the *Steel City Mafia*, a clique of seven, formed in his hometown. They were fearless hustlers that were all about getting money but also were selfless human beings that went above and beyond to do for others what they couldn't make happen for themselves.

Rocking Balenciaga from head to toe, draped in diamond encrusted jewelry, which included a ridiculously expensive Richard Mille, two diamond Cuban link chains, one with a diamond charm that said *El Bichote*, the other with a diamond *Steel City Mafia* charm; flawless diamond studs in his ears, and a diamond pinkie ring, Macho looked like the extremely wealthy cocaine drug lord/trafficker that he was.

Macho's main business was in trucking, much like the family's main business, but he had a hand in plenty of other endeavors. His trucking business was called *Numero Uno Transport* and was comprised of just one truck. He hadn't been too much worried about putting more on the road, though Javi knew that Macho's *Nuyorican* girlfriend and their *Chicagorilla* homegirl had been suggesting it for quite a while. While he was doing the 3-year prison sentence in the Illinois Department of Correction, his woman Yessinia ran his truck, and helping her was her and Macho's homie, G-Baby.

Yessinia Adamari Moralez, was Macho's stunningly beautiful Bronx-born queen. She was a caramel skinned queen, standing 5'9, with the body of a dancer that could check thousands of dollars per night at a King of Diamonds night club. Her long silky hair was the darkest brown, almost black, and fell to her ample ass. The 24-year-old belle was always said to have an uncanny resemblance to the famous Chicago-born Puerto Rican actress, Gina Rodriguez, well-known for her role in the hit TV show, *Jane the Virgin*. What made Yessy one of the most unique women anyone could ever meet, wasn't her incomparable beauty, or her big fat juicy booty, but her extensive military career.

Having been in since she was 18 years old, she had established quite a reputation when it came to being tried, tested, and true. She was currently a *1ˢᵗ Lieutenant* in the army but was soon to become a captain. With time left before she planned to discharge, very likely she'd climb higher in the ranks.

Gabriela Medina, a.k.a G-Baby, was an inch shorter than Yessy, a few shades darker, like maple pancake syrup, with jet black hair. She was just as voluptuous, though, and unbelievably gorgeous. Her eyes were slightly slanted, like an Asians, and her baby hair edges added to her exotic look.

They called her the *Gangsta Boo*, because she was a straight gangster. At 24 years old herself, the Humboldt Park-born and raised gangstress was always ready to box, men and women, she could shoot any gun with precision and was a ride or die chick by very definition. Fucking with her, or Yessy, or Macho, was suicide if it was always up to her when shit hit the fan for them. She was also in the military, with Yessy. She herself had earned rank in the army. G-Baby made it to becoming a second 2ⁿᵈ Lieutenant. With Yessy, they both commanded a *Heavy Equipment Transport* unit, which was a trucker unit charged with transporting all things shippable by truck, to and from bases and camps all over the country, and even overseas.

The two bodacious Boricuas were dressed dapperly in sequined *FeFe Couture* party dresses designed by a close friend of Macho's brother from another mother. The diamond chain that Yessy rocked had a custom diamond charm that said *La Bichota*, and the chain G-Baby rocked had *Chicagorilla* in diamonds. They both sported ridiculously expensive Richard Milles on their wrists as well, and custom diamond choker chains, diamond rings, and diamond bracelets.

They were both inked up with Taino tribals, love for money, guns, and family. The military beauties were known by all as *Macho's girls*, though Yessy was his woman. Nevertheless, people knew that when they saw one of them, the other two were not likely too far away.

"*Maaaaan*, yo, why the freak you ain't tell me you was comin' home, cuzzo?!" Javi asked his cousin as they embraced. "I been hittin' yo' line for the last two weeks and ain't heard shit from you!"

"My fault, lil' cuz," Macho replied, in a velvety smooth baritone voice. "I was dealin' with some personal things that had me in a dark place. I had to get my mind right before I could talk to anyone, 'yah mean?"

"Yeah. I feel you," Javi said.

"It's not a good excuse, I know, to shut out family, but until I was able to deal with my bullshit and not bring around gray clouds, I gotta keep to myself. Good look on tryna uplift me about my raise, though, cutty. That meant a lot to me."

"Somos familia, primo. Yo' moms is missed every day," Javi told him.

Macho nodded his head, then gave Javi another warm embrace. "Happy birthday, youngster."

"Thanks, even though you ain't much older than me," Javi chuckled.

Yessy and G-Baby then stepped up and gave Javi hugs and kisses on his cheek, wishing him a Happy B-day as well. He thanked them graciously, happy to see the two that his cousin loved dearly, and had killed for, many times in the past.

"What's in the box?" asked G-Baby.

Javi missed the sound of her femininely raspy voice; she sounded just like Keyshia Cole.

"Yeah," Yessy added, with her singer-like voice. "Open that shit up, baby boy."

"I forgot I even had this when I saw my big cuz," Javi said, then opened it up.

The circle watched with anticipation. Michelle and Tool were the two that were most interested, since it had come from them both.

"¡Diablos! ¡¿En serio?! Yoooo, this is dope as hell!" Javi exclaimed, when he saw the custom-made charm that was of his Kenworth W9OOL, made of white and clear diamonds.

Some people liked diamond Mercedes signs, or Chevy charms. The Valdez boys, namely Javi, Macho, and their big cousin Danny, were die-hard truck enthusiasts. Javi couldn't think of a better gift that an iced-out Kenworth charm, especially since Kenworths were his favorite truck.

"Maaaan, this is dope. Straight up. Dope!" Javi exclaimed, then he chuckled to himself, looking at it. He held it up high and shouted, *"K-dub gang in this bitch!"*

Tool laughed. "K-Dub club for life, lil' cutty. Your woman came up with the idea for it, then she made it."

ChaCha sucked her teeth. "K-Dub killah! Peterbilts run it, son, but I still love you," she told Javi, hugging him then kissing his forehead.

"Fuck Kenworths," Macho said, twisting his lips. "If you drive one of them pieces of shit, you ain't shit."

They all busted out laughing at the look on Javi's face. Macho grinned at him, taunting him with his wiggling eyebrows. Yessy and G-Baby shook their heads at how competitive the two always got.........just like brothers.

Michelle took the chain from him and had him lean down for her. She put the dripping chain around his neck, then as he stood up, she felt her nipples grow hard at the sight of Dominican perfection.

"Chacho, papi. Me encanta," she told him.

Javi leaned down to kiss her lips, then he smiled warmly at her, making her feel all warm and fuzzy inside.

"I love it, too, mamita. And I love you, to the moon and back."

Javi took her by the hand and pulled her to him, wrapping his arms around her and holding her close. People started taking pictures, capturing the moment that a man and a woman epitomized real love and perfection.

Michelle then pulled Javi down so she could whisper something in his ear. Javi started cheesing up. She took his hand and told everyone they'd be back, then she pulled her man away, towards where a flight of stairs led to ChaCha's loft's private section.

"Wonder where they're goin'," Macho said, wiggling his eyebrows again.

ChaCha shook her head. "Fucking bellacos," she muttered to herself.

CHAPTER 5
STACKS

Stacks was heated. He paced back and forth in Magali's living room, losing his mind. Magali was seated on the couch, tripping as well. Stacks was just about to pipe Magali down, again, when Rambo called to deliver the news of what had just happened with Mikey; Stacks was irate like never before.

"Fuck! Fuck! Fuck! Fuck! Goddammit! What the fuck, joe?" he yelled.

"Stacks... baby... please calm down," Magali pleaded, tears filling her eyes as she started growing afraid of how frenzied he looked.

He whipped his head around and glared at her. "Bitch, this is *yo* muthafuckin fault in the first place! Bringing that gay ass bitch in my fucking circle!" he snapped, walking right up to her.

Magali tried to move away, but he grabbed her by her throat and raised her up. She begged for him to let her go, struggling to breath as his grip tightened. He spun her around and hurled her into the wall hard.

"My fuckin' shitty-booty baby momma flew the fuckin' coop with my daughter!" he continued, pacing back and forth again while Magali sat where she was, in tears. "And now *this?!*"

He got his iPhone out and made a call.

Magali stayed where she was, hoping whomever he was calling would calm him down enough so that he wouldn't hurt her,

"Yeah, man. That little sugar fairy muhfucka I told you about got popped with a *lot* of merch, fam. Shit is finna go *down*, joe! On the Fin! I needs to get the fuck on and get low!"

Magali then gasped, loud enough that it caught Stacks' attention.

"What?" he demanded.

"Stacks… I-I think he still had the gun from the lick."

Stacks closed his eyes and started grinding his teeth as his blood started boiling.

"*Fuuuuccckkk!*" he yelled at the tops of his lungs, knowing that everything he had been trying to make happen, was now seriously fucked.

***

MIKEY

Mikey sat handcuffed to the steel desk, his leg going wild as his discomfort grew more and more by the second. His bowels were full, and close to exploding. All the soft-shellfish tacos with spicy salsa verde on them were threatening to come out very soon, whether he was on a toilet, or not.

Fuck, joe! Where the fuck is this cop at? I gotta shit so fuckin' bad! he thought to himself as he felt pain and pressure constantly building in his gut as if a 500-pound human was stepping on him.

Still dressed in drag, Mikey was more concerned about getting to a bathroom, than all the looks he'd gotten when he was walked from the police vehicle, through the Lake County Jail's booking area, filled with men and women being booked in, and/or trying to bond out, straight towards a hallway that led to the other side of the jail, where the Lake County Sheriff's department had a snitch room.

He was sweating hard, cursing angrily. He still couldn't believe what happened. Rambo had just tried to take him out. He could only imagine what was going on with his sister and Stacks.

The door opened just then, and in came an older Hispanic detective, with a balding head, wearing plain clothes. In his hand, he had a file, of which Mikey knew was his criminal record.

"Sir! I gotta use it! Real bad, joe!" Mikey told him, bouncing around in his seat as he felt one trying to poke through his anus.

The detective ignored him and took a seat across from Mikey.

"Aye, did you hear me? I gotta take a shit!"

The man still paid him no mind.

Mikey started snapping as his bowels came even closer to evacuating. The detective then set upon the table, the Glock 9 that he had used in the Rojas-Gomez dope house lick, to kill one of the girls, and two of his uncle's guys.

At that second, Mikey's bowels let loose. Feces spewed out of his rear end like lava erupting from a volcano. He felt it push out into his pantyhose, caking around his crotch. He was no longer worried about it, though.

He was *fucked*, with no Vaseline.

"Feel better now?" the detective asked, smelling the foul odor as the stench filled the interrogation room.

Mikey looked at him. Tears had welled up in his eyes already.

"So, *Mr.* Miguel Trevino," said the detective, addressing Mikey by his full government name as he opened the thick file to where Mikey's most recent mug shot was displayed. "You have a very long record, *sir*," he said emphasizing the word sir as a taunt. "I am 100% sure you already have a clue what's going on, but just in case you don't, first and

49

foremost, I am Detective Barrera, and I've been assigned to handle this case. You, sir, are in deep shit. Snitching may *not* do much for you, but *not* snitching, you will never see the light of day again."

Detective Barrera studied Mikey for a minute. He saw tears rolling down his face. He knew he had Mikey right where he wanted him.

"Your gun matches what was used in a home invasion out in Winthrop Harbor a few nights ago; the slugs inside of this Glock, match the ones pulled out of a young innocent woman, that was only there to have a little fun, and out of two men. The drugs you had in your vehicle also trace back to what had been the ultimate reason for the home invasion."

"I don't know what you're talkin' about," Mikey said, damn near inaudible.

Detective Barrera looked at the young cross-dresser. "Mr. Trevino, I have your *C.I.* file right here." He held it up for Mikey to see. "You've informed on numerous drug dealers, and gang-members for shootings and all sorts of other crimes. You supplied this information to Detective Gonzalez and were paid." He paused to study Mikey again. Mikey was now looking down at the table. He shifted around, no doubt feeling the mush under his butt and in between his legs, likely dying to get himself cleaned up. "It's nothing to feel ashamed about, young man. Think about it like this: you were helping us clean the streets up, so other citizens that want to live good lives are a little safer. You were influenced by some tough people when you were a kid, and... *touched*," Barrera said, pausing again, looking at Mikey drop his head all the way down so that his chin touched his chest. "So, here's what it is, Mr. Trevino; you haven't been charged yet. The DA isn't even aware of your arrest, because I have not called him to tell him. Your life is *literally* in *my* hands at this moment."

Mikey lifted his head and looked at the man. "W-What do you want?"

The detective smiled like a cat that ate the canary.

"I want to know who you were with when the stash house was robbed and all those people were killed, then I want to know where the drugs, the money, and the guns that were taken from the house are. If you tell me, then they take the fall, and you go on with your life, wherever you want that to be."

Mikey's eyes stayed locked on the detectives for a long awkward minute. He could feel his heart pounding in his chest like Big Foot was trying to kick out of it.

"Or you could try to stay silent, I charge you, then I inform everyone at Statesville NRC, and wherever you end up doing your life-bid, that you snitched on a cartel, and that you like sucking and taking dick in your culo. How do you think *that's* going to play out for you, for the rest of your life?"

Mikey started crying. He just couldn't believe how badly he had just fucked up. He saw Rambo's face in his mind, and as his tears fell, he grew so angry that all he could think of was chopping the guy up into pieces and feeding him to some type of wild animal.

Thinking about it, he still had a lot of coke, dope, and meth left, and he had plenty of money. He knew if he snitched, there would be no returning to Illinois... ever. He'd have to get up with his sister, admit what he did, though he knew she'd find out when Stacks and Rambo went down, then convince her to get ghost with him.

"Okay," he wept, dying to get off his shitty ass and get to a shower and a clean set of clothes. "I'll tell you everything."

Barrera smiled like a pervert that had just committed another heinous act.

"That's very smart of you, sir." He took out his own personal iPhone and went to record the confession. "We'll, uh... keep this all off the books, just so anyone trying to be nosey won't be able to sell you out."

Mikey nodded his head, then got ready to sing like Ariana Grande.

***

CHACHA

Wisin y Yandel's *Rakata* blared as the live DJ kept the festive vibe lit. The bash was jumping; everyone was dancing, drinking, having a ball. Some were on the make-shift dance floor in the middle of ChaCha's lower level, and some were out on the roof-top terrace, blazing exotic strains of loud pack. The ol' heads, Ricardo and Roselyn were all gathered, sharing stories of back when they were all younger, the things they'd experienced during their rise to having money, power, and respect. Javi and Michelle were nowhere to be found.

ChaCha was next to G-Baby, twerking her ass like she was in a music video. G-Baby was making her own juicy round ass clap, competing with the colomborriqueña. Yessy was dancing with her man, and to their side was Tool dancing with Payton, Olivia, *and* the twins.

ChaCha saw the two lovers Evelyn and Gloria, dancing wildly with each other, going *crazy*, in a world of their own.

There wasn't a single person in the spot that wasn't having the time of their lives, while helping Javi bring in the first day of his 25th year of life, and that went quadruple for Javi and Michelle.

***

JAVI

In one of ChaCha's private bedrooms, Michelle was on all fours, face down and ass up, while Javi pounded her from behind. He was sweating his ass off as was she. He'd made her climax three times in a row already, and feeling how wet she was, her pussy farting from so much of her juices leaking out while he went savage on her, he knew she was close to nut number four.

Javi flipped her back on to her back and slid back inside of her through the hole he'd ripped in her pantyhose, once he was on top. He jackhammered the pussy with her legs wrapped around him until she exploded, drenching him again. He came right after her, planting his seed deep inside of her womb.

"Dammit! Did you cum?" Michelle asked him, as he panted on top of her.

"Of course I did. How could I *not*? This toto so fire I could buss' a nut just *lookin'* at it, bae," Javi told her. "And when you wear pantyhose… *maaaan* I can't not go ham on you."

Michelle busted out laughing. "Guess that means I'ma be wearin' stockings a whole lot more now."

"I mean, you can if you want, but you finna be super pregnant, 'cause I'ma keep on bussin' inside this wet-ass pussy when you do. You gon' be the only woman in the world to get pregnant while you still pregnant."

She laughed her ass off again. "Dios mio, este hombre 'ta loco. You keep sayin' that like it's supposed to be a threat, but I can't wait until we have our first child, Javier. You would be the greatest father ever, baby."

Javi smiled, then kissed her lips. "And you will be the greatest mother, beautiful. Ready to go back to the party?"

"Wait. Hold up." Michelle lifted herself up and looked around at every spot they'd gotten wild.

"What is you lookin' for?" Javi wondered.

"Signs of what we did in a room that *isn't* ours. I don't know about *you*, but I don't like bein' on ChaCha's shit list, Javi."

Javi cursed. "You're right; me neither."

They quickly got back dressed and then they cleaned up after themselves. Once they were done, Javi suddenly started laughing his ass off, causing his woman to look at him funny.

"What?" she asked, with a raised brow.

"We're really searchin' this place for cum and booty-skin stains, Michelle."

She busted out laughing again. "Baby, it's your birthday. We can't be gettin' our butts kicked by ChaCha because she finds liquid kids on the floor somewhere in her spotless condominium."

"Good point, but I think we're good, though."

"Then let's get back to the party and act like we ain't do shit but go talk."

Javi laughed. "Bae, everybody knows what we slid off for. Just don't look nobody in the eye, and we'll be aight."

They made their way back to the party, sneaking in with the crowd as Waka Flocka Flame's *Grove St. Party* featuring Kebo Gotti blasted, making the whole condo vibrate. Michelle led her man over to where the bar was and got him the bottle of Moët, she'd had the bartender keep on ice for him.

Javi popped the bottle and before he took his first sip, he poured a waterfall into Michelle's mouth. He took a gulp, kissed her lips, then he took her hand and led her to the dance floor.

***

XAVIER

Half past one in the morning, Xavier, having passed out on the couch in his living room, was awakened by the sounds of Precious's claws, tapping on the kitchen floor, and the sounds of giggling.

He rolled over onto his side and saw that the beautiful red head was giving his dog pieces of ham she'd gotten out of the fridge. Kenzie was dressed in a purple and white stripped tank topped maxi dress-like night gown that went all the way down to her ankles. It fit her *Oh-my-God* voluptuous body like a second skin. She was bare foot, which meant she was comfortable enough to let her feet show.

Beyond her injuries, Xavier could see the tattoos on her arms, and the one above her left breast.

Wow… this girl is the truth, he thought to himself, trying to push the lustful thoughts he was having about her away. She and her daughter were not there for a good reason, and being so attracted to her sexually, made him feel bogus as hell. She was in a terrible situation. She needed a protection, a friend, not a guy that was just trying to fuck on her.

Xavier saw his dog turn her head and look in his direction, as if she could sense that he was no longer asleep. She ran to him and slid to a stop when she was right in front of him. She started licking his face wildly, tail wagging a hundred miles an hour.

"Hey, girl," he said as he stroked behind her clipped ears, which she *loved!*

Precious barked her reply, then nudged him with her nose, as if she was trying to make him get up.

"Okay, okay, pushy. I'm gettin' up," Xavier told her, as he slowly raised himself up from his comfortable position.

***

KENZIE

Kenzie smiled at how Precious was so excited by her human. She could tell she loved Xavier so much. Knowing that dogs knew if a human had a good or an evil soul, Kenzie was again assured that Xavier was likely a dream come true.

She walked out of the kitchen and entered the living room. Sitting on the couch, a couple of cushions away from

Xavier, she glanced at the big TV and saw 50 Cent's hit series '***Power***' was on.

"Couldn't sleep?" Xavier asked her, just as he stood up to stretch.

Kenzie gasped inside when his muscular body flexed inches away from her. His physique had her hypnotized. His big, tatted arms, wide shoulders, deep traps; his six-pack abs so pronounced that she could see them through the tank top he had on. She could not help herself when her eyes roamed downwards to the crotch of his basketball shorts, searching for that print. When she saw it… Kenzie's eyes went as wide as dinner plates.

Good God! How does such a handsome… and very well-endowed man end up rescuing Neveah and me? she wondered to herself.

"Kenzie?"

She looked up and saw him looking down at her.

"Huh? Did you say something?"

He chuckled. "I was askin' if you was havin' a problem gettin' some sleep."

"Oh. Naw. I just don't really sleep that much. I'm weird, but Neveah's out like a broken light bulb."

"All that food she ate, I'd bet. Can I get you anything?" he asked her, as Precious went to her and laid her big head on Kenzie's lap.

Kenzie shook her head. "I'm okay. I just was gettin' some water to wash down some Advil. Precious escorted me to the kitchen, like a professional protector lady."

"She's good at that," Xavier said, looking at his dog.

Sensing that she was the center of topic, Precious lifted her head up and looked at Xavier, wagging her tail again.

"Well, you're welcome to join me watch Ghost and Tommy handle 'bizness, if you want."

Kenzie started smiling as she took another glance at the screen, just as the main star of the show, and his gangster white boy homie were strapping up, ready to go regulate.

"I'd like that, Xavier," she told him.

Xavier sat back down. Precious started nudging Kenzie's left knee with her nose. Kenzie looked down at her with puzzlement. Precious barked, then nudged her knee again.

Kenzie scooted over one cushion closer to Xavier. Precious barked again. Xavier started chuckling.

"Precious let her be," he told her.

But Precious kept on barking, until Kenzie was right next to Xavier. She then jumped up onto the couch and laid across both of their laps.

Wow... this man's dog is trying to make us get close... good girl! Kenzie thought, as she felt warm, rock-hard man next to her, that made her feel so safe, secure, and *aroused*, all in a matter of hours.

Together in silence, they watched the show. Kenzie found it so hard to ignore how attracted to him she was. She'd never met anyone like him. He had such mystery to him, and as she thought about it, she was dying to learn more about the fine cocoa Dominican that had whisked her and her daughter to safety.

CHAPTER 6
JAVI

The bash continued until nearly 6 in the morning. Javi had gotten so many gifts; cash, jewelry, clothes, shades, etc, that he had to have a box truck take it to his house.

"Papacito, somebody wanted to save their gift for last," ChaCha said, as she walked up to him with Vanessa. "It's waiting for you outside. Vamos."

Javi held his woman's hand as they followed her to the elevator. With them, Macho, Yessy, G-Baby, Tool, Evelyn, Gloria, Ricardo, Roselyn, and the ol' heads, got into the elevator and rode down to the main lobby.

"Oh snap! *Eeeeeee*, joe! This me right here?" Javi asked, when he saw what was waiting for him in front of the main doors.

Sitting parked in front of him, a brand-new McLaren P1, sporting glossy blue and black exterior, sitting low to the ground on black rims wrapped in racing tires. The butterfly-style driver's door opened, and the man that had delivered it stepped out, revealing the black Alcantara and carbon-fiber trimmed interior.

Javi and Michelle walked up to the P1 and peered inside. The exotic was *truly* a work of art.

"Aw, yeah. This muhfucka right here off the chain, bae," Javi said.

"It is most definitely a fine piece of European engineering," Michelle agreed.

He took her by the hand and assisted her into the passenger's side, just as ChaCha walked up with her iPhone in her hand. When she handed it to Javi, he saw his big cousin on the screen via video call.

Excited to see his cousin Danny, Javi shouted, "¡Oye, tiguerasoooo! What's up, cuz!"

The 6'4" Danny Valdez, slightly darker than Javi, with dark short cut hair, faded around the sides with *curls-for-the-gurls* up top, and a razor-sharp beard line, smiled at Javi.

"Happy birthday, Lil' cutty," Danny said, with a deep smooth voice that exuded power.

"Thanks, cuz. I appreciate the whip, too. This muhfucka dope!"

"It was built in Europe; special order, just for you."

Javi listened as Danny told him the main three things that had been incorporated into the build. Michelle couldn't help but smile, thinking to herself how not one of the Valdez men took safety for granite.

"Get at me, though, lil' cutty. I gotta go hop in the shower and eat breakfast before I go to my class."

"Fa' sho. I'm still tryna come visit you, man. When you gon' get off that not allowin' us to slide down and let Michelle and I come through? We miss you, cuz."

"Yeah, Danny," Michelle chimed in. "We been wantin' to come see you for a grip now, yo."

"I know, I know," Danny replied, "but I don't want y'all in this environment, or in the system. Once you visit me, you are officially being watched, 'yah mean?"

"Cuz, we ain't worried about it. We just wanna' see you," Javi insisted. "It's been *seven* years since I last saw you!"

"Javi, escuchame bien," Danny said. "I cannot have none of y'all getting any extra attention, just to come sit with me for a few hours. My raise comes because I can't tell ma'dukes *not* to come."

"And ChaCha?" asked Michelle, completely aware that ChaCha was just inches away.

"She's the boss of the business. I *have* to see her," Danny said, after a *very* pregnant pause.

Javi looked at ChaCha and saw how hard she was trying to hide her smile.

"I bet," he said, shaking his head. "Y'all are obvious as hell; you know that, right?"

ChaCha playfully mushed Javi's face with her hand. "Javier, we are just friends, you little punk."

Michelle faked a sneeze. "*Ah-ah- bullshit- choo!*"

ChaCha looked at her and narrowed her eyes. "I'll hit chu' in ya' jaw, cabrona."

Danny's laughter boomed from the phone. "Y'all better *not* piss ChaCha off, yo," he warned jokingly. "Y'all *both* know she's crazy as hell."

ChaCha smirked evilly at them. "They *don't* know, but they'll find out if they keep fuckin' with me."

"No queremos problemas contigo, prima," Javi said, raising his hands up in surrender.

"None at all," Michelle repeated.

"Great. Happy birthday again, baby boy!" ChaCha hugged and kissed his face. "Now gimme my phone so I can talk to my homie."

"*Ah- ah- boyfriend- choo!*" Michelle fake-sneezed again.

ChaCha tried to reach for her, but Michelle hurried and lowered the door closed.

"I know where you live, *cabrona*," she told Michelle. "I'll have someone bring your car home, papacito," she told Javi, then with her phone, she sauntered off, talking to a laughing Danny.

Javi hugged his mother and father, before their non-descript luxury sedan pulled up to take them to the airport. His grandparents knew he and the other two didn't want them to go, but they knew that until things were smoothed over with the government, Ricardo and Roselyn had to stay in the cut, far, far away from the states.

Javi bid adieu to the rest of his people, then got in behind the wheel of his new whip. He put it in drive and pulled off, exiting the valet section onto Wabash. The second he was far enough away from his people, Michelle reached over and started undoing his pants.

"Eeeeee, another one! *Wooo!*" Javi shouted as she freed his dick in less than five seconds. "I'm getting head in a muthafuckin' McLaren nigga!"

"And plenty more to go," she told him, getting up on her knees, and lowering her head down into his lap.

He felt her warm mouth envelop him. His eyes rolled to the back of his head as he came to a red light.

"Happy muthafuckin' birthday to m-m-*meeeeee!*" he groaned, then enjoyed her phenomenal oral skills while waiting for the light to turn green.

***

EVELYN

"Eve?" Nena called out, speed-walking towards her to catch up with Evelyn and Gloria.

In the underground garage, she and Gloria were just about to hop up into Gloria's new Mercedes GL63 AMG truck. Evelyn rolled her eyes when she heard Nena calling her.

"What, *Azalea*?" she asked, calling the Pilsen girl by her government name.

Evelyn turned as Nena approached where she was about to get into the passenger's side of her girlfriend's SUV.

"Um….c-can I ride with y'all? My… car won't start."

"Nena! Why is it every vehicle you fucking touch fucks up?! Yo' car ain't even a year old! *And it's a Benz!*"

"I didn't drive my Mercedes, Eve! I drove my Bubble!" Nena pointed to where the candy banana yellow 1996 Chevy

61

Caprice Bubble she drove sat, one that was re-built by Xavier, sat on 24s, and then given to Nena as a gift. "I don't know what's wrong with it. I just wanna' go home, though."

Evelyn looked at her. She knew Nena was bullshitting. She had helped Xavier build the Chevy in his garage; she knew for a *fact* that nothing was wrong with it.

"Get in, Nena," Gloria told her, shaking her head, "and just so you're aware, I am not stopping past Xavier's house."

Evelyn looked at the girl and could tell she was salty about that.

"Oh… um… maybe I just need to press the gas pedal when I turn the key," Nena said, then without another word, she took off, running to her Bubble.

Evelyn shook her head again. "I am really gonna smack the shit out of that girl one day. Dick-thirsty-ass hoe."

She and Gloria got inside.

"She is *too* damn thirsty," Gloria said as she started the supercharged AMG-built V8 engine. "That's why Xavier would never wife her ass up."

Evelyn laughed her ass off as Gloria put it into drive and pulled out, pulling past Nena, literally just sitting behind the wheel of her car, staring off into space.

***

XAVIER

Xavier woke up and discovered that Kenzie was laying on top of him, sleeping soundly and peacefully. They were still on his couch; Precious was laid out on the floor. Sitting next to her with the remote to the TV in her hand, was Neveah, in her butterfly-print pajamas.

Kenzie's eyes opened just then. She realized that she was laying on him and gasped, getting up off him like he was a hot griddle iron, burning her skin.

"Oh my God! I am so sorry!" she told him, eyes wide with shock.

Xavier chuckled softly, then gave her a re-assuring smile. "No harm done, ma. At least you look well-rested."

She sighed. "Somehow, I slept *really* good."

"The comfort of real muscle will do that for you," Xavier replied, then looked over at Neveah. "Good morning, little lady over there."

The little girl looked over at him, then she jumped up and ran over to him, right into his arms. Precious jumped up and ran over to him as well.

Kenzie was flabbergasted by how her daughter had run into Xavier's arms. Xavier was even surprised by it. Kenzie had never seen her daughter gravitate to any man, not even her own father.

"Aw! Thank you, Neveah!" Xavier said to the little angel, hugging her back while Precious stood next to her, tail wagging excitedly. "I'm gonna have a super good day at work now, all because of this super hug from a super little girl!"

Neveah giggled, then she let him go and climbed up onto her mother's lap. Kenzie cradled her daughter in her arms and kissed the top of her head, then she got up with Neveah and started flying her around like she was a little plane.

Xavier's heart was warmed by the sight. He had a lot of respect for women that went the distance to be good mothers to their children, no matter how hard life might be for them. He saw Kenzie as the prime example of that.

"Do you work, Kenzie?" he asked her.

"Yeah. I'm a teller at the bank in the Wal-Mart down the street from here."

"Oh, okay. You need to go in today?"

She shook her head. "I took a leave of absence, until I figure my mess out."

Xavier nodded his head in understanding. "Okay. Well, it's fine with me if you stay here while I get to work, or... you and Neveah *could* ride with me, if y'all want?"

"What do you do?" Kenzie wondered, having been wondering since she rode in his fly-ass SUV, and slept in such a majestic home.

"I'm a truck driver."

Surprised by that, she asked, "Like, one of those big 18-wheelers?"

He nodded.

"Wow. Drivin' a truck gets you a house this nice and a Range Rover that's dope like that?"

He shrugged with a smile on his face. "I work hard for what I have, and I have a lot of fun doin' it, 'yah mean?"

"I wanna' go, mommy!" Neveah pleaded. "Can we go? *Pleeeeaaaase?*"

Kenzie laughed at her little girl. "If he's really okay with it, then I am."

"I am," Xavier told her. "I enjoy havin' company when I'm on the road. Precious comes with me, too, most of the time."

"Okay. Well, I guess we're goin' for a ride, then."

"Cool. Let's get showered, and we can pick up breakfast on the way to the yard," Xavier suggested, then he got up and took Precious to the kitchen, to get her fed and watered before he did anything else.

***

VICTOR

"*Why?*" he snapped, after Diablo reported to him, that although he had followed Javier Valdez and his woman in a new Rolls-Royce from Chicago, back to Lake County, he had not made a move like he was supposed to. "People always shoot at each other on the damn E-way, *cabron!*"

"I do not endanger innocent people in my line of work, Victor. And plus, I was only really doing recon," Diablo told him. "When I strike, it will be to where I catch them *all* in one spot."

"You don't think that they *were* all in one spot?!"

"Maybe. It's not like I could get in, though," Diablo informed him. "My source says that the Valdez queen owns the building they'd gone into, and the security guards there are all ex Special Forces, Rangers, Navy Seals, and Marines, and they all had some serious artillery. There'd have been *waaaaay* too much to handle at once, and too many innocent people would have died; I'm a killer, not a monster."

"You sound like a bitch!" Victor snapped.

Diablo laughed. "I know you're upset, so I'll let that slide. But just so you know, you're all over the news getting the shit beat out of your ass, on camera, by a woman. So, feel free to never call *me* a bitch again."

"Just do your fucking job, *pendejo!*" Victor demanded, then he ended the call, tossing his phone up onto the dashboards of his new Lingenfelter-edition Corvette ZR1.

Barrera called as Victor was about to pull off from his parking spot.

Victor grabbed the phone and answered it. "You better have good news."

"Actually, I do." Barrera told his nephew about the arrest of one of the stash house robbers, and how he made the young dude flip and snitch on the two leaders of the four-man crew, and his own sister.

"Wow. He's ruthless," Victor said, shaking his head. "I have something for his ass."

Barrera started laughing his ass off. "You might wanna re-phrase that, nephew."

He told Victor why.

"Fucking joto," Victor grumbled, again shaking his head. "I gave him a phone to use, though; it has a tracker in it."

"He'll toss it and run, tio," Victor told him.

65

"I know, which is why I called Death in on it as well. The little puñal has had eyes on him ever since he stepped out of the jail… dressed in that shit-stained dress. He made a call to his sister, and she's on the way to pick him up as we speak."

Victor perked up at that. "Are the other two with her now?" he asked eagerly.

"No. An undercover unit's tailing her, though. My guess is, she'll pick him up, they'll go to wherever they've got the rest of the stuff stashed, and then they'll try to flee. But they won't make it. Mr. Trevino has no clue, but he isn't the only loose-lipped pinche *mierda* in the circle."

Victor started smirking at that. "Good job. When we find the other two, I am going to personally slice their fucking stomachs open and make them watch their own intestines fall out, then I'll blow their heads off, then I can really focus on those pinche Valdez fuckers."

"You and that family." Barrera chuckled. "Hope you know what you're doing, nephew."

Barrera ended the call.

Victor put his phone on the charger. "Of course I do, you old fucker. I am the master at this shit, bitch! This is *my* state! Illinois is *mine!*" he proclaimed, then he pulled off, to head to the private airport in Waukegan.

CHAPTER 7
STACKS

Eeeeeee, joe! Shortie thick as fuck!" Stacks thought to himself, as Rambo turned from off Lewis Avenue, into the Burger King parking lot.

Rambo wasn't exactly thrilled to be literally across the street from where he'd just blamed at Mikey's SUV. Still, being right where he was just shooting at less than 24 hours ago had him on edge.

Stacks told his guy that there was nothing to worry about, since they were in Rambo's candy-red 1998 2-Door Chevy Tahoe, sitting up on chrome 26" Vellanos.

Stacks' eyes were right on the fat juicy ass of a light-brown skinned chick in a short and tight-ass skirt, as she had hopped out of an exclusive big body BMW. He noticed the Root-Beer candy-painted Cadillac Escalade it was parked next to, sitting on massive rims that were much bigger that what he and Rambo rolled on.

Next to the Escalade, he saw a gleaming white Bentley Flying Spur, also sitting on chrome rims. Stacks surmised that the thick red bone was meeting up with whoever was pushing the 'Lac truck and the Bentley. His mind *instantly* went into lick mode.

"Joe, you see that bitch, fam?" Stacks asked his homeboy, as the chick entered the Burger King.

Rambo parked the Tahoe a few spaces away from the side entrance. "Hell yeah, I do. She bad as fuck, but I bet she goin' in there to meet up with whoever ridin' that Caddy truck and that Flyin' Spur. Whoever pushin' them is *gettin'* it, joe! On the *Five!*"

"It could be some hoes pushin' them muhfuckas, bruh. If it is, joe, we finna slide on them and see what they holdin'," Stacks said, trying to see into the establishment's tinted windows.

"And if it's some dudes?" Rambo asked, killing the engine.

"Then they finna be our next stains," Stacks told him, and opened his door to get out.

***

MICHELLE

Creep-ass niggaz! Fuck is y'all lookin' at?!" she thought to herself, seeing the dark-skinned and the light-skinned guys staring into the windows at Evelyn, as she made her way to where she was sitting at.

"Hey, sis!" beamed a happy dominicana, as she made her way towards her.

Michelle's eyes were still on the two guys. They were entering the restaurant, still looking in Evelyn's direction, with obvious mischief on their minds.

"What up, ma?" Michelle stood up and hugged Evelyn, while she kept an eye on the two men, whom were now in line to order.

Noticing Michelle's tenseness, Evelyn released her and asked her what was wrong.

"First, you need to start being waaaaay more aware of your surrounds, baby girl. ChaCha told me about what happened at that gas station down the street; you should be on guard whenever you out and about; you forgot who you are?"

"No." Evelyn looked a little salty that ChaCha was telling on her. "I never seen a picture of dude, though, Michelle. I didn't know who he was."

Michelle nodded her head. "I understand. Just be aware more; you haven't noticed those two dudes eyin' you like some perverts 'n shit? No me gusta esa 'mielda, yo."

Evelyn turned and looked at the men that Michelle was talking about. Neither of them were looking their way now.

"Fuck 'em. They don't want no problems," Evelyn said. "I'ma go order, though; be right back."

***

STACKS

Stacks grinned as he peeped the thick light-skinned chick coming his way. He and Rambo had already ordered, and were standing to the side, waiting for their meals. One person had been behind them, ordered just an order of large fries and a pop, then left. They ogled the girl as she stepped up to place her own order.

Staring down at the girl's big booty, Stacks' dick started getting so hard that it pulsated in his Polo boxer briefs. He licked his lips and pictured himself bending her over and fucking her hard from the back while he pulled her hair.

"Aye, yo!"

He and Rambo both were startled when they heard someone snap. They turned and saw an unbelievable beautiful woman there to their right, looking so good in the tight-fitting light and dark brown Fendi dress, monogrammed with F's all over it. It fit her like a second layer of skin.

Her dark-colored hair was in four big braids with tiny little braids in between them, going to the back. Flowing down from under her form-fitting dress's mid-thigh length hem, were the silkiest smooth legs they had ever seen. On her feet were light-brown low-top Fendi sneakers.

She rocked diamond jewelry that they both knew was all flawless and had to cost a grip. They figured if she wasn't the one driving the Bentley, then she was pushing the Donk'd Cadillac truck.

"You wanna' stop eye-fuckin' my lil' sister like she's a piece of meat, yo?!" the beautiful chick snapped, with a New York accent, as the light-skinned chick turned and looked at them, with a frown.

"Whoa, lil' mama," Stacks said with a grin. "Be cool with that attitude, joe."

Light skin stepped up to him, as the employees back behind the ordering counter all stopped working, hearing the commotion going on.

"Don't talk to my fuckin' sister like that, mamahuevo!" she demanded, cracking her knuckles. "Debes tener un deseo de muerte, hablando con mi hermana como si estuvieras *loco*."

Stacks and Rambo were both surprised when the girl spoke Spanish.

"What the fuck you just say, shortie?" Stacks asked, with furrowed eyebrows.

The beautiful chick in the denim dress spoke up for her. "She *said*, ya dumb-ass must have a death with, talkin' to her sis like you crazy."

Stacks grinded his teeth in anger. He was about to raise his hand and pimp-slap the shit out of both the smart-mouthed hoes when he heard the door open again. He and Rambo looked and saw three light-skinned men enter, all three of them rocking designer swag and iced-out jewelry.

One was shorter than the other two; compared to the other two bone-crushers, he had a more athletic physique but still looked like he was a very strong man. In his long hair, he had neat zigzag braids that hung down to his chest, with a razor-sharp baby hairline and beard, with green eyes.

The second tallest was *very* muscular, like a heavy-weight boxer. His Iverson braids reached down to his wide barrel chest. His baby hairline and beard were also razor-sharp. Like Green-eyes, he had colored eyes as well, but his were bluish-gray eyes. Stacks noticed that along with the diamond herringbone-style chain around his neck, he had a diamond charm that said, *'Steel City Mafia'*.

The tallest of the three had to be at least 6'6 or taller, with broad shoulders, huge arms, wide chest, had long dreadlocks. He too had a diamond chain that had a Steel City Mafia charm.

All three of them looked pissed. Their faces told Stacks and Rambo that there was about to be some smoke.

Rambo immediately caught the vibe and could tell that the men were not people that he and his guy wanted to tango with.

Green-eyes walked right up to Stacks, standing toe-to-toe with him. The Burger King employees and people that were eating, all had their phones out, recording the altercation.

"Check it out, my man. That's my baby sister you bumpin' yo gums at and the other chick is my lady," he told Stacks, glaring right into his eyes. "Apologize for the disrespect, or you and yo guy finna get rolled up in this bitch, joe. What's it gon' be?"

"Lord."

Stacks felt Rambo touch his shoulder and attempt to pull him back. "We got moves to make, joe. Let's be out."

Stacks shook Rambo's hand off him and shot a venomous glare right back into the green-eyed man's eyes.

"Ion' give *no* fuck, lord!" Stacks snapped. "Fuck these pussy-ass mutha-"

WHAM!

Stacks sentence was cut short when Green-eyes' woman rocked him in his jaw as hard as she could. Due to how short

71

she was to him, she had to jump up to catch his jaw, but she did it, and Stacks fell to the floor.

"¡Hoy te jodieste con las personas *equivocadas*, mamahuevo!" she snapped, and started stomping and kicking him.

Rambo saw the light-skinned chick advance on his guy to get her some. He charged at her and was about to snatch her up by her hair, when faster than his eyes could even process, Iverson Braids ran up on him and got on his bumper.

BINK! BINK! BINK! CRACK!

Iverson Braids hit him with a lightning-fast 4-punch combo, following up with a devastating right hook, laying his ass like Tyson did Spinks in the 90's.

Rambo flew backwards and hit the floor, seeing two of everything.

Stacks hurried to get up before the girl could kick him again. Her foot came flying right as he got up to one knee. He grabbed her leg and was about to pull her legs from under her, but she yanked her leg out of his grip and planted the soul of her shoe in his jaw.

Stacks ate the blow as he rose to his feet. He went to jab the denim-dress chick in her face, but she ducked it. He missed by a mere inch.

Green-eyes rushed him and started swinging furiously, delivering three fast left-right-lefts. Stacks jumped back, eating the punches and got on his guns. He and Green eyes started boxing like they were in an alley, in a circle, fighting to the death. The dread head went to where the ladies were and pulled them behind him, while Iverson Braids stayed on Rambo.

He picked Rambo up off the floor, and raised him up over his head, looking like a braided-up Hercules, and tossed Rambo over the counter.

Green eyes got the best of Stacks, taking a few punches in his face and head, but countering with more that had more effects on Stacks. A hard right hook did it. Stacks went down, hitting the floor, everything around him spinning.

He felt himself being picked up, then he heard, *"Bums away, muthafucka,"* then the next thing he knew, he was flying, over the counter, landing hard on top of someone else. He heard Rambo groan from under him.

"Yeah bitch! ¡Habla esa 'mielda ahora! ¡MMhuevo!" he heard one of the women shout.

***

JAVI

"Alrighty, then, little mean girl," Javi said, scooping his woman from off the counter, after she'd climbed up onto it and screamed down at the two that laid on the dirty floor behind it. "Sis! Let's go! Now!" he then told Evelyn.

"But I didn't get my-"

"Now, sis!" Javi hollered, then whisked his woman and his sister out of the Burger King, ignoring all the phones recording them.

***

MACHO

He walked up to the counter, where the young Latina manager stood, still stuck where she was, dazed by his bedroom-blues.

"Sup, gorgeous? Lemme' get two Number 2s, with a large Sprite and a large Mountain Dew. And while I'm at it," he said, pulling out a wad of Big Face 100s, and tossing it to her, "lemme' go on 'n get that video footage of what just happened here," he added, giving her a million-dollar smile that made her feel like she was about to melt right there next to the two beat-up guys.

73

CHAPTER 8
MICHELLE

She was dying laughing at the whole thing as Javi tailed his sister's BMW, heading north up Lewis Ave towards Zion. In the back, Diamond barked excitedly, while Demon sat quietly, snorting and grunting.

"Yooooo, bae, I swear on everything I love, you and Macho are nuts!" Michelle laughed, as she had to yet again wipe the tears of laughter from her eyes.

"*We're* crazy?" Javi questioned with a chuckle. "You are the one that socked buddy up and got to stompin' his ass at the register."

"He deserved it. Fuckin' creep-ass was all starin' Eve down 'n shit! I hate that shit when dudes do that, yo!"

Coming up to the intersection of Lewis and Beach Road, the light was red. Javi and Michelle heard the V12 under Evelyn's hood scream out as she mashed the gas pedal to the floor. She blew through the red light, leaving her brother sitting there.

"Okay?" Javi said to himself, with a raised eyebrow.

Michelle laughed. "She is a mini ChaCha, bae."

"Don't I know it," Javi replied, chuckling as Diamond's nose nudged his right elbow.

He turned around and gave her big head a pat, then rubbed behind her ears.

Michelle's iPhone dinged as the light turned green. She pulled it from her monogrammed Fendi handbag as Javi rolled onwards. Looking at the screen, Michelle gasped, then she cursed out loud.

"¡Coño! Javi! That was him!" she shouted, looking at her man.

"Who?" Javi asked with furrowed brows.

She showed him the picture on the screen that popped up from the '*Vic-Alert*' app she had on her phone, that picked up signals from phones that belonged to targets she was searching for.

"That was the guy that Xavier asked us to handle! That's Kenzie's baby daddy!"

Javi's jaw dropped. "Shit! Yo, call cuz and see if he saw where dude and his guy went!" he told her, whipping his steering wheel hard to the left, spinning his 'Lac truck in a 180-degree spin in the middle of the street, about-facing, and mashing the gas pedal to the floor.

The monstrous supercharged V8 engine under the hood roared as Michelle hurried to get Macho on the line.

"Yo, what up? Y'all gucci?" he asked when he answered.

"Macho! The dark-skinned dude... *that's* Kenzie's baby daddy, cuz! The one Xavier wants us to get! Is he still there?" she yelled so that he could hear her over the loud engine.

"Naw, lil' cutty. Him and his mans dipped up outta here in and hopped in a red 2-door Tahoe. Me and bro finna go catch they ass right now. They went up Yorkhouse Road."

"Catch them! Whatever you do, catch that muthafucka!" Michelle yelled before ending the call.

"Bae, get the sweeper from under Diamond!" Javi hollered over to her, as he flew back down Lewis to get to Yorkhouse.

Michelle made her female Cane Corso move and after she unlocked the secret lever. Hurrying, she lifted the seat up, got the fully-automatic Heckler & Koch G36 from the secret hide-away gun rack that was already loaded with a 100-

round drum, full of 5.56mm rounds and readied herself to get rid of Kenzie's problem… forever.

***

STACKS

"On Vicelord, joe! I'm finna kill all them bitches, lord!" Stacks yelled angrily, as Rambo pushed his Chevy truck west on Yorkhouse Road, passing up the entrance to Bevier Park, with the small 4-way intersection for Yorkhouse and McAree Road a minute up from where he was.

Rambo was seething with anger. He'd never been so embarrassed in his life.

"Lord, those *had* to be them Dominican niggas we supposed to be hittin', too! On Ghost! That was them, joe!"

"Fam, we gon' see they asses real soon! All hands on deck with this! I'm finna call Magali and make her put her people on gettin' me locations stat!"

Rambo approached the intersection and started slowing down, when he saw a flash of white in his rear-view mirror. He glanced up into it and saw the white Bentley coming, *fast*.

It jumped over into the on-coming lane, forcing the two vehicles that were heading in the opposite direction off the road. Rambo's eyes went wide in shock, when he saw the big dread-head in the passenger's seat stick the business end of a shotgun out of the window.

"Oh shit, lord!" Rambo shouted in panic.

He slammed on the brakes just as the Bentley pulled right up alongside his door, but the driver hit his brakes, too, and skidded into the lane in front of him.

Stacks hurried to get his gun, just a moment too late.

BOOM! Aaagghh, fuuucckk!" Rambo screamed, as a blast from the 12-gauge sailed through the door and tore into his left side.

"Lord!" Stacks shouted in panic.

BOOM!

The dread head hanging out of the Bentley's passenger window blew the pump again. The blast hit Rambo in the side of his head. It exploded into pieces, flying all over Stacks' face.

"Shit!" Stacks yelled in shock, eyes wide with horror as he looked at his long-time brother from another mother's headless corpse, sitting behind the wheel, the nerves in his body making it jump and twitch as if he was still.

In a last effort to save himself, Stacks ducked low and reached over, grabbing the column shifter and slamming it into reverse. He reached his foot over and mashed the gas pedal down, just as the dread head and his brother jumped out of the Flying Spur with their guns.

The Tahoe shot backwards. Stacks gripped the steering wheel, poking his head up to look out of the rear window. Shots flew through the windshield, coming so close to hitting him. He yanked the steering wheel to the right and spun The Chevy to the left, about-facing to head back the way that they had come after fleeing the Burger King. He slammed it into drive and mashed the gas pedal again, shooting off with the corpse still right there, blood spewing out of the neck stump.

But as he shot back east on Yorkhouse Road, Stacks' heart dropped when he laid eyes on the same Escalade, that was at the Burger King, heading right in their direction. And standing up through the sunroof, pointing a machine gun right in his direction, was the beautiful girl that had kicked it all off.

***

MICHELLE

"Dddiiieee muthafucckkkaaa, diiiieeee!" Michelle screamed as she squeezed the trigger to the big military-grade *SAW.*

The H&K G36 spit so many rounds at the Tahoe, hitting the grille, flying inside the cab area. After nearly fifty shots, the Tahoe veered to the right and hopped the curb onto the grassy side of where Bevier Park was.

Seeing Macho and Tool in the Bentley, hurrying to catch up with the Tahoe, Michelle held on as Javi followed, hopping the curb and continuing to chase the Chevy truck down, ignoring that it was broad daylight, and they were seconds away from residential areas.

Michelle sank back down into the Cadillac truck and kept her eyes on the vehicle. Ahead of it, there was nowhere it could go. It was heading right for a big pond that was where Waukegan's annual fishing derby was held.

But to her surprise, the Tahoe didn't slow down. It kept speeding through the grass, heading right for the large body of water.

"What the fuck?" she heard Javi say.

Then, the Tahoe sped up an inclined hill and went airborne, flying high up into the air before plunging into the pond with a massive splash.

"Heeeelll naw, joe! ¡*Que se joda*!" Javi said, slamming on his brakes right as he got to where a little building sat at the edge of the parking lot. "Gimme the gun!" he told Michelle urgently.

She gave it to him. Demon and Diamond jumped out with him and ran to the pond where the rear end of the Tahoe was bobbing up and down like a buoy. Michelle hopped out with two automatic Glock 18s and joined her man and the dogs at the pond's edge.

They both pointed their guns started firing, side by side. Javi dumped at the SUV; Michelle aimed at the fuel tank. She hit it, and the Chevy truck exploded.

Javi continued blowing his big gun, shooting round after round into the water around the half-burning SUV, taking extra measures in case somehow, one of them got out and swam away.

When the whole drum was empty, Javi stayed where he was for a good long minute, assessing the area. He looked for bubbles in the water, movement of any sort. After a whole 60 seconds of not seeing anything, he and Michelle turned and hurried back to the 'Lac truck with the dogs right behind them.

In the middle of the parking lot, Macho and Tool were posted in front of the Bentley, both now with shotguns in their hands.

Michelle jumped up behind the wheel as Javi got in the passenger's seat after getting the dogs back into the rear.

Just then, the sounds of screeching tires got all their attention. They all looked and saw two Waukegan police Impalas speeding into the parking lot with their strobes flashing and sirens on.

Javi, Michelle, Macho, and Tool, didn't move. They stayed where they were, how they were, and waited as the two cop cars entered, and skidded to a stop.

Before the cops got out, the ones driving pointed at the four Dominicans, instantly recognizing them. They both dipped up out of there without a second to spare. The Valdez family goons were very well-known, not only to the streets, but to the law. *Nobody* willingly sought smoke with them, because they were too hot to handle.

Michelle put the Escalade into drive and pulled off, throwing the deuces up at Macho and his brother on the way out of the parking lot. They both nodded and got back into the Bentley to follow them out.

Javi called his brother on speaker as Michelle banged a left turn onto Yorkhouse Road and mashed the gas pedal to the floor.

"Dimelo, 'mano," Xavier said as he answered.

"Tell lil' mama *Hakuna matata!* Dude and his mans went *bye-bye!*" Javi told him and ended the call.

79

Michelle busted out laughing at him as she stopped at the stop sign at Yorkhouse and McAree, grabbing her iPhone as she heard it ding from an e-mail.

"You are funny as hell, Javi," she told him, glancing down at the e-mail, rolling onwards.

Javi chuckled and turned around to praise their dogs for being on point.

"Ooooo! Bae! I gots another job! This one's gonna be *fun!*"

"Aren't they all fun for you?" Javi asked her. "Like that crooked-ass lawyer in downtown Waukegan we took out with his cum-guzzlin' secretary?"

"*More fun!*" She handed him her phone so she could see it.

Javi looked at the job and saw what his woman meant by *"more fun"*. "Oh yeah....*this* is right up your alley, amor. You gon' need some help?"

"Baby, you are *always* welcome to ride with me, because I am *always* gonna ride with you. Now, we're gonna go past the yard, to your office, because I am so fucking horny from all this shit, and I still owe you like... a hundred blow jobs."

Javi busted out laughing at his woman. "¡Dios mio, esa tipa 'ta loca!"

***

XAVIER

Xavier walked back towards where Kenzie and Neveah were standing at the front of his chromed-out heavy-hauler Kenworth W900L. The mother and daughter duo had stayed posted at the front of the ridiculously expensive Oversize-Load carrying rig. Next to them was Xavier's trained female *Dogo Argentino*, whom he had named Precious. Coming back towards them, from just ending a call, Kenzie saw the smirk on his face. She could tell that something big had just happened.

He came to a stop right in front of her and took her hands into his. "Your worries are over, ma," he told her, looking down into her eyes.

Registering what he meant, Kenzie went wide-eyed. "You... you mean..."

Xavier nodded. "He *can't* bother you, or nobody else, ever again."

Sighing, Kenzie picked her four-year-old daughter up into her arms and held her. For a minute, she was silent. Then her eyes started welling up with tears.

Kenzie and Neveah were the newest additions to Xavier's and Precious' life. Kenzie was a statuesque Cuban Armenian-mixed belle with mad body, and the reddest hair ever.

African American father, whom had been an abusive son of a bitch to Kenzie like it was completely okay to hit women, especially women that was the mother of his child. Neveah was an angelic little brown ball of joy to Kenzie, and to Xavier. To Kenzie's surprise, her daughter had taken to Xavier, and responded to him like *he* was her father, instead of Stacks.

Xavier had taken the two into his life, when after a hot little fuck session with one of his honey-dips, he had been leaving out and discovered the red-head in the lobby of the apartment building. She looked terrified.

It took a little encouraging, but eventually, Xavier got her to roll with him. He wasn't exactly sure why, but he knew if he didn't offer to help the obviously petrified woman and end up hearing later one that the body of a woman with fiery red hair was found somewhere in Zion, he wouldn't know what to do with himself.

As time went by, hanging with the two ladies, Xavier felt himself growing attached to both, and it made him wonder why, because he was definitely the type to switch chicks like kicks and not think twice about it.

"You okay?" Xavier asked her, taking her hand into his.

She shrugged. "I never want bad things to happen to anybody, but... my daughter's life means more to me than my own. I just wish it didn't have to end like that, Xavier."

He smiled at her, admiring how she had such a big heart, that she felt bad that her baby daddy was dead, despite how badly he did her, physically and mentally. He found it to be a very noble thing.

"You reap what you sow, Kenzie. Personally, I'd have rather caught him and beat him up a few times, but a guy that points a thumper at the mother of his child... he would *never* have stopped until you were the one takin' a nap forever," He nodded his head at Neveah, who laid calmly against her mother's chest, "and then *she* would be without *you*."

Kenzie understood exactly what he was saying, and she agreed. Though she didn't want her baby daddy to have to die for her and her daughter to live peacefully, when it came to him, or her, she chose *her,* and her daughter. She lived for her little girl, and nothing else.

"Enough of the clouds, though, ma. You two ready to roll?"

Neveah turned her head and shouted, "YEEEAAAH! LET'S *ROLL!*" she quoted excitedly.

Chuckling at her daughter, Kenzie kissed Neveah's cheek, just as she saw a silver big body BMW pull into the yard, with a little piglet's snout pointing up out of the open passenger's window.

***

EVELYN

"Goddamn! *Another* one?" she asked herself when she saw her brother in front of his heavy-haul truck, with a thick chick that was holding a little girl in her arms, and Precious.

Evelyn got a good look at the woman as she rolled past. She was dressed in a red V-collar shirt, with a pair of old 80's style high-waist acid-washed skinny-leg jeans, and on her feet were white flats. Her hair was up in a messy bun, and the only makeup she wore was red lipstick.

"This nigga got a muhfuckin' *white* bitch at that, too? With fake ass and titties? Bro trippin' hard now." She started smirking as she turned into a spot next to where her big Volvo 780 was parked. "Wait 'til Nena hears about this," she said to herself then.

Her piglet started squealing as he dropped down from trying to see out of the window.

"That's right, baby!" She scooped Oinky up into her arms and kissed his snout. "There's gon' be some real live drama in the *Dedicated* Truckin' yard real soon! ¡Chacho, papa!

***

VICTOR

"What the hell?! And the fucking cops didn't arrest them?!" Victor asked, bewildered by the news.

"I'm beginning to think that you haven't grasped the true, shall I say, nature of who you are dealing with," Detective Barrera told him. "Have you ever actually stopped to think of why your father has never *once* gone at it with the Valdez brothers?"

"Yeah! Because he's fucking soft!" Victor snapped at his uncle.

Barrera laughed. "HA! Your soft father never got his ass kicked by a chick in a gas station!"

"Whatever, tio. Hey? Whatever happened to that little puñal that was involved in hitting my spot up?"

"Oh... he's being used to find what remains of the money and drugs he and his crew hit you for," Barrera told him. "As for the others, one is dead; got his face blown off by a shotgun during a chase in Waukegan."

Victor laughed. "Live by the gun, die by the gun, eh, tio?"

His uncle laughed. "Indeed. The other one, whom the little pip squeak said ran the crew, he was with his dead friend, but the divers haven't found his body yet."

"Divers?" Victor asked.

"Yeah. They were in an SUV and took a plunge into the pond at Bevier Park. Crime scene is still there at this moment. Funny thing is it all started at a Burger King. The two got their asses to them, by whom I discovered were, guess who......Ding! Ding! Ding! ¡La Familia Valdez, cabron!" Barrera shouted theatrically then.

Victor twisted his lip as his uncle laughed his ass off.

"Then that's when things got taken to the streets," he concluded. "But for the little joto once his purpose is served, he will have his wish granted."

"His wish?" Victor questioned.

His uncle told him what was to come of the little cross-dressing homosexual that had been a part of the crew that had hit one of Victor's main stash houses, and made off with enough cocaine, heroin, opioid pills and guns, that he and whomever he had been with likely because overnight celebrities. Before they had left, they killed everyone inside, even a few innocent girls that were just there to party.

"Wow... that is *demented*," Victor said, then he suddenly busted out laughing.

"You're laughing now," his uncle spoke, "but what do you think those Valdez people will do to *you* if you keep messing with that kid?"

CLICK!

Victor ended the call. "¡Chingate, *puto*!" he said suddenly angry.

He called to his new secretary through the call-comm on his desk.

The short petite Guatemalan woman entered his office in less than two minutes. She was wearing a red tight-fitting cheetah-print Donna Karan wrap-dress with long sleeves and a low cleavage line. Her legs were encased in sheer black pantyhose. Red 5" heels were on her feet, giving her 5'3" frame a few more inches in height. Her hair was up in a ponytail, she wore red lipstick, gold hoop earrings, with a gold necklace and a gold ladies Gucci watch. Framing her beautiful face was a pair of red glasses with gold Gucci symbols on the sides.

"¿Si, jefe?" the sexy woman asked, with a certain look on her face that said she was already thinking she knew what he wanted.

But, instead, Victor put her on business.

"I want you to go and apply for a job at Dedicated Transport," he told her, *completely* shocking her.

Her jaw dropped in shock. "Seriously? You're going to keep trying them, boss?"

"What the fuck did I just say?" he roared, shooting up out of his chair, with a fiery rage in his eyes that almost made her shit on herself. "Do what the fuck I tell you por I will chop you the fuck up and feed you to your fuckin' kids!"

Penelope shook her head, then chuckled. "As you wish... *boss*," she replied, very sarcastically, then left out, without closing the door behind her.

"Stupid bitch! I shoulda' made you suck my chile first! Wait 'itl you get back, slut; I'm fucking your face *and* your ass! *Bitch!*" he cursed, then he sat back down and stared at the ceiling.

CHAPTER 9
MICHELLE

Michelle turned a right onto Frontage Road and stayed in the left lane, coming upon the yard seconds later. Through the fence, Javi saw his brother's heavy-hauler rolling towards the exit, then it made a wide right turn out onto the road as Michelle came to a stop in the left-turn lane.

Xavier tooted his loud air horn at them as he made the turn with his longer-than-normal big rig. Michelle beeped and waved. As he shifted gears and put the pedal to the medal, she and Javi caught a glimpse of the red head and her child in the passenger's seat.

"Aww! Bae, they look good together, yo," Michelle said, smiling at how happy they had just looked.

Javi nodded his head. "Bro does look happy; I haven't seen smiles like that whenever he's with Nena, or the other ones."

Michelle turned into the yard. They saw Evelyn behind the wheel of her big metallic green 780, backing up to the 53'-foot long luxury enclosed 6-car-carrier trailer. It was emerald green like her truck, with gold letters spelling out the company name, the *D.O.T* and the *MC* numbers under it, along with the dispatch location and her business phone number.

Gloria was there as well. She had just gotten out of her Mercedes SUV, after she'd parked next to her black and silver 2-tone T660, which also displayed the company info in silver letters on both sides of the big spacious 86" midroof-style sleeper berth. The T660 was already coupled to an identical car-carrier, which matched in color to Gloria's truck.

Olivia and Payton, were in their rigs, heading towards the yard's exit. The twins, Kiara and Jada, were also in their trucks, which were also 10 car transporter Peterbilt's, following Olivia and Payton to exit the yard and get on the road.

All the 10-car haulers that Evelyn had were built with 3-car racks built onto the tractor; two vehicles could ride on the rack that was above the cab, and the little box-shaped sleeper berth, while one could ride on the section that was right behind the sleeper, over the tractor's rear wheels. It was coupled to a green steel open-rack-style trailer that could carry up to seven more vehicles, depending on their size.

As the four ladies rolled past where Michelle parked at the office's main entrance door, they tooted their air horns at the big boss and his lady before exiting out of the yard.

Tank, O-Boy, and Bull, were all in their trucks, waiting for Javi. The six others were already gone, with six of Javi's dry-van box trailers.

Tank's big 2001 Freightliner Classic XL was a favorite among many truckers. It was one of the few that a man of such size could fit in, and be comfortable in, for days on the road. It was perfect to fit the massive 400-pound Samoan, who stood at 6'9" tall.

O-Boy was in a Kenworth W900L like Javi's, and Bull was in a 2005 Peterbilt 379 Extended Hood. They were all part of Javi's crew, though everyone that drove a truck for Dedicated Transport worked for Javi. He was the owner but had broken his company into three divisions-*Exotic Auto/Domestic Transport*, that he put his sister in charge of, and the *Specialized/Oversize Load Transport* division of which he had put his brother Xavier in charge of.

The three ran the show, hauling high-dollar freight nearly every day, but their bread and butter came from all the *highly illegal* goods they all hauled for Javi's long list of underworld clients and associates.

Javi, Michelle, and the dogs got out of the Cadillac truck. His Kenworth was still outside, but he could tell someone had washed it. It was gleaming in the bright sunlight, as if it had just come out of the wrapper.

Javi got to it, getting on his pre-trip inspection. While he checked his rig over, Michelle and the dogs headed over to Evelyn's truck.

Gloria stood to the side while Evelyn was connecting her air and electrical lines. In her arms was the Notorious P.I.G, of which Evelyn had named Oinky, snorting and grunting happily.

"Oinky Woinky! Hey, there, cutie!" Michelle cooed, nuzzling his nose with her own, making his tail wiggle.

Demon and Diamond sat down, but were looking up at the piglet, trying to figure out what the furry little thing was.

"How's everything been goin' with you, mami?" Gloria asked Michelle. "Eve told me what happen at the Burger King; I swear to *God* I wish I was there."

Michelle nodded her head. "It's all good, ma. It's handled. Life goes on, feel me?"

Evelyn turned around after her lines were connected and looked at Michelle.

"Why did y'all turn around?" she asked.

Michelle told her that the dark-skinned man that Javi threw over the counter was the guy that Xavier wanted dealt with. She told her what had transpired from that point on, which put shocked looks on both ladies faces.

"Goddamn! Yo, Javi is a muthafuckin' G for *real*!" Gloria then said, looking over at where Javi was just closing the engine hood to his truck.

"Bitch, get off of my brother's dick!" Evelyn jabbed, putting her hand up in Gloria's face right as she was about to snap back. Evelyn looked at Michelle and said, "Y'all ass went through all *that*, for a bitch that Xavier's just gonna' fuck and leave?" she asked, with a raised eyebrow, "a *white* bitch at that?"

"Evelyn." Michelle gave her a stern look. "Do *not* start that shit."

Evelyn scoffed, but didn't argue. She didn't want to piss of Michelle. *Nobody* did.

"Anyways," Michelle continued. "Is y'all rollin' together, or goin' separate ways?"

"Together forever!" Gloria leaned into her woman and kissed Evelyn's lips. "We got a contract with a guy that owns a few luxury and exotic auto dealerships. He got new building built, and we're picking up his inventory from the old spot in Chicago, to take to the new dealership in Libertyville. Then we gotta go grab the ones from his place in Naperville that are going to another spot in Palatine, and Lake Forest."

"Easy money," Evelyn added, as she took her piglet from Gloria.

"Hey!" Gloria whined.

"¡Callate, bitch! He's *my* oinker! Get yo' own, hoe!"

Michelle laughed her ass off at the two. They acted just like Javi and Macho, when they went toe-to-toe.

"Aight, yo. You two be safe, and Eve." Michelle looked at her. "Use your eyes a little better," she said, then hugging them both, kissing Oinky's snout, she and her dogs headed back to re-join Javi, just as he started up his truck's engine.

***

MAGALI

"Aww, what the fuck, joe! You fucking stink, Mikey!" Magali exclaimed, when her disheveled cross-dressed little brother got into the front seat of her 2005 Mercedes S500. "You smell like shit!"

"That's yo' punk –ass car, bitch!" he shot back, salty as he adjusted himself on the leather, sore from dried feces caking up around his ass. "Fuck is you snapping on me for?!\ I just got out the fuckin' jail and you going in on me like that, joe!"

Magali pulled off from the front doors of the Lake County Sheriff's department, heading south to get to Belvidere Road. Tears had dried around her eyes, which were puffy, and red. Mikey looked at her and saw her face.

"Sis? What's up?"

Magali sighed. "Stacks is dead," she told him, "and so is Rambo."

Mikey's jaw dropped in shock. "H-How?"

"Shot. It was on the news; some people were chasing them on Yorkhouse Road, shooting at them. Rambo somehow crashed into the pond at Bevier Park. They only found Rambo's body, though; he was burned beyond recognition because whoever was shooting shot the fuel tank, and it blew up in the water." She came to the light at Belvidere and made a right turn. "The news people said the Tahoe was hit so many times that there was no way anyone else that was in it could've survived. They got divers searching the pond."

Mikey's eyebrows furrowed. "He could still be alive if they didn't find his body."

"Stacks can't swim, and even though they literally have no actual suspects, the word on the street is some Spanish-speaking people that looked Black beat them both up in Burger King, then somehow ended up hawking them down and dumpin' on them."

"Spanish-speaking Black people?" Mikey gasped. "You think it was those Valdez people?"

Magali shrugged, digging under her seat and pulling out a bag with a quarter ounce of white powder in it, handing it over to her brother

"All I know is shit is *waaaay* too hot to stay around here, so we need to get gone. I got a quarter mil' at my crib, and I still got coke, dope, and some ice."

With glee, Mikey opened the bag, dug his long pinky finger in it and scooped out a mound, snorting it up like it'd disappear if he didn't. He powdered the other nostril, then noticing how much more powerful it was than what he had, he threw his head back and snorted hard, forcing the sour dripdown his throat.

"Woo! Mmmm!" he squeaked, as he instantly went numb. "Shit! Damn that shit is fi', joe! I got three bricks of coke at my crib and about $15 grand; go to my crib, I'll get everything, and we can go."

She nodded but said nothing. Instead, she glanced up into her rear-view mirror and saw the big black Chevy Silverado 3500 dually pick-up truck behind her. She did her best to hide the smirk that threatened to give away her charade, and kept her eyes on the road, while Mikey snorted more of the heroin-laced cocaine that she had put together, just for him.

***

KENZIE

With the jake-brake on and roaring out of the big exhaust pipes, Xavier down-shifted gears, slowing his heavy-hauler down as he merged onto the exit ramp at Exit 333, in the town of Sturtevant, of Racine, Wisconsin.

Kenzie was getting goose bumps from the roar; having never been inside a semi before, especially one as nice as Xavier's, she found herself to be having the most fun ever, just riding with him, her daughter, and Precious.

Glancing over at him, she couldn't help herself but to bite her bottom lip as he gripped the wood grain steering wheel with his left hand, and had his right hand on the shifter, constantly breaking down gears on the declining exit ramp. The fact that he was so carrer focused and took his shit serious turned her on something serious She willed herself to stop lusting for him, before she ended up creaming her panties. On top of not feeling like he would want her anyways her daughter was there.

Precious laid on the shiny wood floor in Xavier's 63" flat-top style sleeper berth, which was so luxurious that Kenzie was astounded by it when she had first climbed up inside the truck. It was as comfy and deluxe as a luxury sedan, with a powerful sound system wired around it.

***

XAVIER

Kirko Bangz's *Drank in my Cup* bumped as Xavier made his way around to get to the heavy machinery dealership. He made two right turns that led him to a 2-way street that ran along I-94, where he'd just came off.

The gigantic business came up on his left. Xavier made a wide left turn into the loading/unloading area for trucks. Right away, he saw Thurgood's black and chromed-out Peterbilt 389, and Pete's 2014 Kenworth W900L. Both of their rigs were coupled to hydraulic RGN Low boys that had four axles and could carry 60 tons like Xavier could.

They were both parked, side by side in the loading/unloading area, along with five PJ& D heavy-haulers, and heavy-haulers from other companies.

Xavier turned the music down as he began hearing chatter on the CB.

"Ooooooweeeee, look at that sexy-ass Large Car that just came up in this joint, yo! All shiny 'n shit!"

Kenzie and Neveah both looked over at Xavier, seeing him laughing. He knew the voice very well.

Grabbing the mike off the CB's hook, he replied to the familiar voice.

"That sounds like the *Bad 'Rican*! Is that you, big cuz?" he hollered out, heading back to the big turn-around to about face, and get parked next to Pete.

"¡Ya tu sabe, muthafuckaaaaaaa! Wooo! ¡La *'Riqueña mala* y *La Gangsta Boo* up in this *biiiiiitch*! What's goodie, yo?" he heard Yessy reply.

"Comin' to get a little bit of this money with y'all, cuz," Xavier told her, making a big left U-turn and rolling into the spot next to his mans. "I don't see that pretty Legacy Class that big cuz got, so what truck is you in?"

Yessy's voice came back as Xavier parked his rig, putting the shifter into neutral applied the brakes, then grabbing his iPad to put his trip log onto *'On-Duty/Not-Driving: Loading'*.

"Gabi and I stole one of ChaCha's trucks; we in the baby blue 379 a few doors down from Thurgood. We're hoppin' out right now; see you in a sec."

Xavier hung his mike back up and looked over at Kenzie, seeing her and the youngster looking at him, with puzzled looks.

"You are about to meet *the* wildest Puerto Rican chicks ever right now, ma," he told her, just as Precious got up and stretched her legs.

"Is that a good thing?" Kenzie asked.

"It is when they're not your enemies," he told her. "Come on and hop out with me, gorgeous," he added, then patting Precious's head, the three got out of the truck.

Precious jumped up onto Xavier's seat and watched out of his open window, seeing the two bodacious Boricuas walk up to Xavier and the ladies, right as Thurgood and Pete walked up, dapping him up.

She barked out of the window at them, her tail wagging excitedly as she remembered exactly who Yessy and G-Baby were.

"Girl yo ass better stop barkin like you want some smoke, Precious!" G-Baby yelled out to the dog.

"She misses Maliante and Dreams," Xavier said to G-Baby. "And it's been a grip since she been around Pablo."

"ChaCha only brings him out in public when someone's in trouble, or when she needs security that won't fail," Yessy said. "That dog is a demon dog."

Xavier chuckled, then he introduced Kenzie and Neveah to Yessy and G-Baby. Kenzie was wowed by the two beautiful women. They had an aura about them that made her excited to be in the in presence. Even in work clothes, the two were stunning.

Her long hair was in two braids to the back, the tails balled and scrunched up at the nape of her neck. She was dressed in a neon-blue work shirt with *Numero Uno Transport, LLC* on the chest, with dark blue skinny-leg jeans, and sky-blue Timberlands on her feet.

G-Baby was wearing a baby-blue Numero Uno work shirt, black skinny-leg jeans, and black Timberlands on her feet. Her hair was braided in twelve little cornrows to the back.

Both had their ridiculously expensive Richard Milles on their wrists that were each worth more than a two brand-new Bentley Mulsannes, and they rocked diamond choker chains around their necks, with big Chanel hoop earrings in their ears.

Kenzie couldn't believe women that looked like them drove trucks. They were so thick and beautiful that she wondered why they weren't on stage shaking all that ass they had for tons of cash at the most popular night club in the country.

What she didn't know, was that Yessy's boyfriend was a certified cocaine drug lord, and a high-level drug trafficker, as was Javi, Evelyn, and Xavier. Being tied in by years of putting in work, and years of close friendship, G-Baby couldn't be any closer to the two, if she was related by blood.

Kenzie had no clue that the life of a truck driver could be so eventful, and profitable. It damned near made her wonder, just for a second, if she had picked the wrong career field.

"Neveah?" Yessy asked Kenzie. "That's Heaven spelled backwards, right?"

Kenzie gasped. "Yes! Oh, my God! Nobody has ever figured that out before!"

"She is adorable!" G-Baby squealed, crouching down and taking one of Neveah's hands into hers. "Hi, Neveah! I'm Gabriela! You are so beautiful!"

Shyly, Neveah smiled, trying to bury her face in her mother's leg.

"Say thank you, baby," Kenzie told her.

"Thank you," the little girl said to G-Baby.

Xavier reached for her and scooped her up into his arms, making her giggle when he raised her up high into the air.

"Well, how about we go inside and make our presence known?" Thurgood suggested, ready to get to it.

Following him in, they all entered the big dealership building to get the paperwork and keys to the machines they were all picking up.

CHAPTER 10
MIKEY

After a long shower, and dolling himself up in drag once again, with makeup on, then doing his hair, Mikey leaned down and snorted two more lines from the bag that his sister had given him. He threw his head back and snorted it all down, enjoying the re-energizing back-drop. He went and sat on the toilet, and groaned as the euphoric bliss made his dick hard.

He was so high, feeling so great. As he sat there, he began nodding off, slobbering on his dress.

KNOCK! KNOCK! KNOCK!

Mikey jumped when he heard the banging on the door. He wiped the drool from around his mouth and wiped away the snot beginning to ooze from his nose.

KNOCK! KNOCK! KNOCK!

"*What?*" he shouted when the knocking came again.

From the other side of the door, he heard his sister yell, "*Hurry the fuck up Mikey, we gotta go!*"

"Bitch, I'm comin'! Shut the fuck up!"

He hurried to tie the baggie back closed, then he looked in the mirror once more, checking himself out. He smiled and blew himself a kiss. He had no problem going out in drag now. There was no more Stacks, nor Rambo, and his sister had seen him dressed in drag so many times. They'd gone on double dates together while he was in his *mode*.

"Mikey, come the fuck on, pinche punål! he heard Magali shout again.

"I *knooooow* this bitch did not just call me a fag!" Mikey said to himself.

The high-heeled stiletto boots he wore clacked loudly on the floor as he stomped towards the door, ready to punch her right in her mouth.

Snatching the door open, Mikey was ready to fight, when he locked eyes with a man. He was brown-skinned, with long hair, and a scar on his face. He was dressed like a rancher that was about to go to a bar for drinks. His eyes were dark and soulless specs.

Mikey's heart nearly dropped out of his ass when he saw a tazer in the man's hand.

"Wh-Who-"

POW! ZZZZZZZZZZZZZZZZZZZZZZZZZZ!

Mikey dropped the floor when the man popped his ass and sent 100,000 volts of electricity through his little body, making bowels evacuate, *again*.

***

MAGALI

"Fucking nasty-ass dick-sucker!" Magali shook her head as she watched her brother shit and piss on himself, while he convulsed on the floor.

Diablo released the taser's trigger. The young boy was incapacitated on the floor. A big brown and yellow puddle had pooled out from under his dress. A rank odor immediately filled the air, invading his and Magali's nostrils.

"Good job, chula. You'll be rewarded greatly for your participation," the head sicario told her, fanning the air in front of his nose. "Holy crap, this little guy stinks!"

97

He ordered the two others he was with to get Mikey tied up and into the van they'd driven behind his big black Chevy dually pick-up truck.

"¡Hijole chingao, patron! ¡Este guey se cagó en su... vestido!" one complained, tortured by the foul stench.

"So, what! Try to hold your bowels while you get tased and tell me how that goes for you! ¡Callate guey y ponlo en la camioneta!"

Magali smiled at how demanding the old school hit man was. "Daaaamn, papi, you're a boss for real, eh? I love that shit!"

Diablo chuckled as his men started bounding Mikey's ankles and wrists with duct tape. One stuffed a sock in his mouth and put duct tape over it, then put an old potato sack over his head.

The second one pulled out a vial with clear liquid in it, and a new syringe. He sank the needle into the soft top, pulled the plunger up to get the needle filled with the liquid sedative, then he injected the dazed cross-dresser in the neck, sending him off to La La Land.

The man that lifted Mikey up grumbled angrily. "¡Pinche *sucio* puñal!"

The two left out of the apartment then.

Magali went and got everything her little snitching brother had stashed. She returned to Diablo's side minutes later. She handed him the big plastic bag with the drugs and cash in it.

He looked at her for a minute, then he shook his eyes.

"You keep it. You've earned it; working with me, chula, you're gonna earn so much more. Let's get on our way. We've got more work to do, then you can come with me down to my mansion down in Monterrey and get *fuuuuuucked* up with me, eh?"

Magali smiled, nodding her head excitedly. "Sounds good to me, guapo. Let's go."

They hurried out of the apartment and got to where his big black 3500 series Chevy pick-up sat idling, just as his two men pulled off in the windowless van, they had Mikey tied up in.

***

MICHELLE

She laughed her ass off as Javi and his guys talked shit to each other on the CB, while they were heading south down I-294, passing through Northbrook.

Javi, O-Boy, Bull, JB, EZ Money, Cadillac, Sergio, Pistols, Black, and Tank, were all turning and burning, all of them with empty 53 foot long dry-van trailers coupled, ready to be loaded with the high-dollar freight that Javi had booked for them all.

Most of them were going to be heading down to southern regions of Illinois, while a few were going west out of Illinois. Javi, himself, was going to Joliet. The coke his brother, sister, ChaCha, and himself had brought from Jersey, was ready to be transported to the trusted clients of the Valdez family. This time, Javi had a *lot* of security going along. There was no more toleration for attempted ambushes or hi-jackings.

Having his beautiful killer, and the two murderous Cane Corsos along for the ride, Javi felt like he was the safest human in the world. He needed no other back up but the three of them, but of course, he knew just the four of them wouldn't exactly be enough if Victor Gomez so happened to learn their whereabouts and sent more clowns at them.

"Aye, Tank!" came O-Boy's voice from the CB radio. "Aye, joe! If yo' motor was as big as you, *booooooy*, yo' ass would leave us in the dust, famo! On *BD!*"

Javi and Michelle busted out laughing as Tank spoke to get back at O-Boy.

"Maaaaan, get cho' '*I say I'm from Chicago but I'm really from Vernon Hills*' face-ass on up outta here! Lookin' like you wanna be *Like Mike!*"

Javi grabbed his mike from his Cobra to hop in the roasting. "Aye, Boy! I *knooooow* yo' ass ain't gon' let him call you lame-ass Bow Weezy, fam! Yo' ass better get '*iiiiiimmmm*!'"

Michelle heard O-Boy's response come a second later.

"Tank! Yo' ass look like a giant Mexican!"

She and Javi laughed even harder.

"On my momma, joe!" continued O-Boy. "I'm finna flame yo' ass, joe! Ooooooo, you look like a 600-pound George Lopez!"

They kept getting on each other's bumper until I-55 came up. Javi bid them all adieu, then switching to the Stevenson Expressway, he shot south to I-355, then took it to Joliet.

Arriving at the big plant, the gates opened for him to ride right in. The armed guards in the shack and standing around it all nodded their heads and waved to him. He tooted his train horns back and headed to where he was to get loaded.

Michelle rubbed behind Diamond's ears as her head rested on her lap, while Demon sat next to Javi. Michelle looked out of the windshield and watched all the movements of forklifts, other trucks, cranes, and workers walking to and from wherever. It made her smile, being in a relationship with someone who came from such a prominent family that became heavies in virtually in every venture they dove into.

Javi rolled towards another gated section, with a sign that had '***Danger: Restricted Area. Authorized Personnel Only***'. Up ahead of them, Michelle saw the red X-edition Peterbilt 379 Extended Hood, but next to it, she saw another one that was the color of Jade and sported as much chrome and stainless-steel as the X-edition. Both flashy Peterbilt's were coupled to 53 foot dry-vans, both with diamond-shaped Hazardous Material placards with the numbers *1778* on them. Backed to the loading dock with their swing doors opened, they were soon to start getting loaded with high-dollar freight.

Michelle and Javi then saw the drivers of the two rigs standing off to the side, talking to the plant's supervisor.

"Oh snap! Cuzzo ridin' with us?" Javi asked out loud, sounding shocked when he saw Macho next to ChaCha.

"Isn't he on parole?" Michelle asked, looking at the braided-up drug-lord.

"I would think so, if he just got out a few days ago," Javi said, reaching the center of the turn-around and turning his steering wheel to the left to bust a big U-turn. "Knowin' him, though, he probably gave his parole agent a big bag of money to forget about him until it's time for him to sign those discharge papers."

Michelle laughed as Javi about-faced, came to a stop, then shifted into reverse. He backed his rig to the dock, softly bumping up against it seconds later. He put shifted into neutral, then applied the brakes.

Looking to her right Michelle saw ChaCha's massive tiger-striped Dogo Canario sitting on her seat. He looked like a giant tiger-striped Great Dane with a Pit Bull's head, with his clipped ears and strong muscular jaws.

"Aww! Bae, she brought Pablo with her!" Michelle blew the big Presa Canario kisses through the window.

He stood and started wagging his tail. When he barked, Diamond and Demon both barked.

"His ass got so big since I last saw him, yo," Michelle said, as Pablo stuck his huge head out of the window, sniffing at her.

Diamond stood up and placed her front paws on Michelle's lap, then barked at Pablo, tail wagging excitedly at the Alpha Male dog of the Valdez family. Pablo barked excitedly, leaning further out of the window.

"Okay, now, you two. No mixing of breeds. I want purebred Cane Corso puppies, Diamond, not Cane Canario pups," Michelle said.

Javi laughed. "Let's go see what goodies we shall be hauling around the Land of Lincoln today, love," he told his woman.

They both got out, leaving the dogs in the Large Car to communicate with Pablo. Walking up some steps to the dock, Javi and Macho dapped each other up, as the ladies hugged. The plant's supervisor, an older African American woman was greeted like family by Javi and Michelle.

"I got you all ready to be loaded up, Javier," said Tabitha. "Come on up in 'hea and see what cha' got."

She took them into the loading dock building and showed them so many pallets of plastic-wrapped kilos of cocaine. It looked like when *National Geographic* showed a federal drug holding facility.

"Eeeeeeee, so many bricks!" Javi exclaimed, then started rapping, "All white bricks! So many bricks! Rappers talk abot it but ain't never seen this!

Three forklifts drove out from a corridor and got to it when Tabitha called them via her 2-way radio.

Javi and Macho chopped it up with each other, while Michelle and ChaCha talked girl talk.

Each trailer was filled halfway with ten pallets containing five hundred kilos each, then the last half was filled with pallets that were stacked with plastic 55-gallon drums, filled with water, though marked with hazmat placards displaying that the liquid was sulfuric acid. The highly corrosive acid was chosen to be the front, because most cops were lazy, and not many wanted to go through everything that was needed to be able to check the entire load, should they pull one of the three over for a random inspection.

Besides, the security that was riding along with each truck would deflect any interference in delivering the product, by any means necessary.

"Anything on Bitch-tor Gomez, prima?', Javi asked ChaCha.

"Not from what I've heard. My mole told me he's been busy handling the people who hit his stash house. One of them, a little cross-dresser, got caught up and they are doing him *soooo* dirty. The other two are dead. I guess they got shot at in Waukegan and ended up plunging into the pond at Bevier Park."

Michelle and Javi both gasped in shock, then they looked at each other.

"Wow... this is a small-ass world, yo," Macho said, chuckling.

ChaCha looked at them quizzically. "Talk," she then told them.

Javi told her about Kenzie's baby daddy and what had happened.

She shook her head. "Well, my mole knows that Victor Gomez has an uncle that's a detective in the Lake County Sheriff's office. There aren't any suspects reported."

"I bet," Macho laughed, remembering how the cops that had arrived on scene were so scared when they saw them all with their guns, that they dipped up out of the parking lot like a plane was about to crash land on top of them. "Fuck the po-lice, yo."

"By the way," ChaCha said, "I need a favor from you, Javi."

"Name it," he replied.

ChaCha told him what she needed. He and Michelle looked at her with furrowed brows.

"Are you for real right now?" Javi asked.

"Yes. It's part of my plan, papacito."

"How do you know you can trust her?" Michelle asked. "What if she's acting like she's working *him*, but really workin' *you*?"

ChaCha looked at her. "Because she's been paid $100k, and she knows how painful her death would be if she fucks up."

"Hmmmm... good point," Javi chuckled, knowing that people that killed like ChaCha were a dime a dozen.

People that got on the colomborriqueña's shit list, there was literally nowhere on earth they could hide, that she wouldn't find them.

"Okay," Michelle then said, "but, yo, if the bitch even shows even a tiny hint of bullshit, word on my motha', yo she's Diamond and Demon food."

ChaCha laughed. "As long as they save some for my big papi in my truck," she said, thinking of how her dog loved raw bloody meat.

Once all three trailers were loaded, ChaCha made a call, getting the Rastas on point, and the greedy dirty Chicago cops and Illinois state police she had on pay-roll ready to work.

CHAPTER 11
JAVI

"Cuidate, primo," Javi said to his cousin through the CB, as he rolled towards the plant's exit behind ChaCha.

Macho replied, "Ya tu sabe, cabron. Te veo despues."

Outside waiting, there were twenty vehicles waiting outside the plant, in the lot across from it. Javi saw Jamaica sitting in a late 90s Mercedes-Benz CL600, with a chrome Superman emblem in the grille. The rest of his crew were deep as hell in BMWs, Cadillacs, Chevies, and GMCs. Half a billion dollars' worth of coke was in each trailer. Pedro and Diego made strict demands to the Rastas: *No* fuck ups, at all.

Javi's iPhone rang as he came to a stop behind ChaCha, as she waited for the gate to open.

Answering Jamaica's call enthusiastically, Javi shouted, "¡Tio, wha-gwan, shotta!"

He and Michelle saw his smile as his laugh came out of the speakers.

"Rude bwoi! Ya' ready to get a little richa', mon?" the top dread asked.

"Yessir! Ready to go make these drop offs, B! 'Yahm 'shayin!" Javi replied, imitating Money-Makin' Mitch from *Paid in Full.*

"Me 'ear 'dat, little shotta! Wha-gwan wit' 'de rude gyal?"

"Hey, Jamaica! It's all good, yo! 'Bout to 'git it, B!" Michelle hollered out.

"Shizzl! Let's boogie, 'mon!" Jamaica then said and ended the call.

***

EVELYN

Down in Chicago, close to Lake Shore Drive, Evelyn, Gloria, Payton and Olivia arrived at the exotic auto dealership at a quarter after 9 a.m. The employees had already started parking the vehicles along the street to cut time in getting them loaded. Ferraris, Lamborghinis, Bugattis, Audis, Porches, McLarens, Benzes, Beemers, Bentleys and Rolls-Royces made the street look like a huge collaboration of mega rap stars was about to be filmed there.

Evelyn got parked, put her log onto '*Loading*', kissed her piglet's snout, then leaving the windows down and the a/c on for Oinky, she got out to go meet the business owner.

With papers for each vehicle in the first four loads in her hand, Evelyn handed the ladies the ones they were taking. She and Gloria would transport the more exotic and higher end vehicles in their enclosed luxury trailers, while Payton and Olivia could carry the less expensive and easier to fix vehicles on their open-rack style trucks.

Gloria got two very rare and stupid expensive Mercedes CLK GTR Lemans racers, valued at over a million dollars each. She also got one of the very last Dodge Vipers made, with three Bugatti Veyrons.

Evelyn got a Lamborghini Aventdaor LP-700, two Lamborghini Gallardo LP-570s, a Porsche Carrera GT, a Ferrari LaFerrari convertible, and a Koeniggsegg Agera R, something that most rich people won't even get to see, except for on a *Need for Speed* movie.

Payton's and Olivia's trucks and trailers were loaded with top-of-the-line Mercedes, BMWs, and Audis.

The ladies got each car loaded, applied their emergency brakes after taking the keys out with them, then strapped and/or chained them down. In just under an hour, the four were ready to pull off with the first loads of many more to go.

Sitting in the driver's seat of her Volvo, Evelyn was tucking her paperwork into her clipboard, with Oinky sitting on her lap, when a call from her big brother interrupted her music.

She answered excitedly.

"¡Heeerrmaaannoooooooooooo! ¡Dime lo que *pasoooooo*, tiguere!" she shouted to him.

Javi's chuckle came through the speakers of her cab and sleeper, while Oinky looked around curiously for where it was coming from.

"Why you so turnt' up, sis?" Javi asked.

"Because my brother is such a cutie pie, and I love him so much, and I'm happy he's calling me!"

He laughed. "Well, alrighty, then! Baby sis just made my day! I was callin' to let you know that we gon' have a new face in the office."

"I know. ChaCha told me about 'Nessa. Xavier's gon' be *too* geeked, bro! Straight up!"

"Oh yeah. There is most definitely gon' be some love in the air. I'm not exactly sure how that's gon' play out with his new friend Kenzie… or Nena… or his other honey-dips."

Evelyn sucked her teeth. "¡Que se jodan *todas* esas putas, bro! Vanessa is who he needs to make his wife. On big cuz Tommy!"

"That's for bro to decide on, Eve, but I wasn't talkin' about 'Nessa."

Evelyn's eyebrows rose up in confusion. "Who are you talkin' about then?"

Javi told her the situation.

"¡Vete! Are you serious right now?" Evelyn asked, shocked. "How do we know that the bitch ain't two-timin'!"

"That's what I asked, but ChaCha's response to that was irrefutable. Cuzzo know what she's doin', and I trust her with my life."

"Okay," Evelyn sighed. "You're the boss, bro, but if I catch the bitch on some snake shit, she gon' accidentally end up gettin' hit by my truck."

"I believe you." Javi laughed. "We got her covered, though, sis. Just keep yo' eyes open, 'cause shits crazy right now."

"Claro, 'mano. Thank you for earlier, too, bro."

"Ain't shit. You're my baby sister. You already know what it is. Love you."

"I love you, too, you green-eyed cutie pie fucker."

Javi busted out laughing, then ended the call.

Oinky stood up on his hind legs and put his snout to the bottom of Evelyn's chin. She giggled and leaned down to kiss his face.

"Well, we got a new bitch comin' to work at Dedicated, Oinky boo. If she even looks at you wrong, you and me, we finna beat that bitch up! You with me?"

Oinky looked up at her and snorted.

"Cool. Let's get this show on the road, papi," Evelyn told him, then set her clipboard up on the dash, grabbed her iPad and started her drive time again.

"Aye, *Booty-Full*?" came Gloria's voice, calling Evelyn by her CB handle.

Evelyn grabbed her mike and replied, "What do you want, *Glory-Hole*?" she asked, calling Gloria's by her own handle.

"Fuck is you doin' up there? We ready to go!"

"Shut up, bitch! *I* run this shit!" Evelyn shot back.

As she hung her mike up, Evelyn heard Payton's voice. "Y'all are weird as hell."

"Ya momma's weird, hoe," Evelyn replied, as she clutched into 1st gear, and she released her brakes.

Olivia's laughter came through the CB just then. "You been around Macho too much already, Eve," she said, as it was known that Macho always got on someone's mother when you pissed him off.

Evelyn busted out laughing as she pulled, leading her ladies away from the dealership, with her piglet on her lap, and her music back on and bumping.

***

XAVIER

An hour after arriving at the machinery spot, Xavier had a used Caterpillar 345 C excavator loaded onto his trailer, chained down, the outsides of the two caterpillar crawler tracks flagged, to mark how far they hung over the 9'-foot wide Low-boy trailer, and had big yellow banners with Oversize Load in black letters on the tractor's front bumper, and the rear of his trailer.

Weighing 900 pounds short of 100,000 pounds, Xavier had a mighty heavy load to carry, that would net him a cool $15,000, for just a few hours of a drive south to Missouri.

A pilot vehicle had arrived to escort Xavier and his over dimensional load down to the massive road construction site. It was too wide, too tall, and too heavy to not need one.

"Ready to go, ladies?" Xavier asked Kenzie, Neveah, and Precious as he put the paperwork for the machine on his clipboard.

"Yeess!" shouted Neveah excitedly.

Precious barked.

Kenzie nodded her head, with a smile that was more flirtatious than she meant it to be.

Xavier smiled back at her, then he clutched his transmission into 1st, released his brakes, radioing to the pilot car driver, telling him he was pulling out.

***

JAVI

Macho split off with his motorcade escorts to shoot north where he was delivering his yayo. Javi and ChaCha's first runs were right to Chiraq. Javi went and dropped off 1,000 bricks to an older Dominican businessman that owned a popular auto detailing spot in Humboldt Park.

ChaCha and half of the escorts shot out west, to take 2,000 kilos to a large group of *Solid* hustlers that had a big storage facility off California and Harrison.

After Javi got back rolling, he took Sacramento down to Madison, hit a right and rolled over to Pulaski, where he dropped off 4,500 bricks to one of his family's biggest distributors in Chicago.

ChaCha successfully made her first drop, then she bent the corner and hopped on the E-way, shooting out south, heading to *Mo-Town*. At a car rental agency, she dropped off a whole 7,500 bricks to an old school coke mover that had ties all around the Midwest *and* Canada that flocked to him like seagulls fighting over slices of bread at a beach.

Javi took the last of the coke he had to a man that was waiting behind a movie production studio on Sacramento. When he arrived there, the guy had two box trucks and a crew to get everything unloaded. He was a major player in the world of cocaine, and supplied many actors and actresses, along with screen play writers that loved nose candy, with Grade A product.

With empty trailers, Javi and ChaCha headed back to the plant for another load. Macho pulled in after them. They all got loaded with another half billion dollars each, then shot north, delivering to various cities and towns, until they were all empty, and back in Lake County.

***

EVELYN

On their second run up from the city, Evelyn and the ladies made a stop for fuel at a diesel station in Highland Park, right on the side of Route 41.

After she topped her tank off, she let her piglet out to stretch and use the bathroom. She then went inside to use the bathroom herself, as did Gloria, Payton, and Olivia.

Somehow, Evelyn got selected to buy everyone a beverage. She grabbed everyone's requests from the coolers and went to stand in line.

In front of her, an old man that was buying so many cartons of cigarettes that she could smell the tobacco. It almost made her vomit.

"Excuse me, miss?" she heard from behind her.

Turning around with a raised eyebrow, and the warnings from ChaCha, Michelle, and Javi in her mind, her hand rested on her pocket, where she had a butterfly knife. But when she saw whom had spoken to her, she nearly gasped.

He was the most handsome chocolate-complexioned man she had ever seen. The guy was giving her a prize-winning smile, with a mouth full of pearly whites.

He stood at least 6', with a fresh bald-fade haircut, and a neat low-trimmed bread line. His physique was athletic; the black t-shirt with Balenciaga in red letters fit his upper half tightly, while the red leather Balenciaga shorts, he had on gave him a retro edge that she was digging. Down on his feet, were black Balenciaga Arenas, with red laces.

The diamond chain around his neck, she could tell was real, as were the diamond studs in his ears, and the diamond Rolex on his wrist.

The cologne he wore wafted into her nostrils, making her mouth water.

"Hey, I'm sorry to disturb you," he said, with such a smooth baritone voice that it started to stir up a feeling in the lower regions of her body that a man had not been able to do in a *loooong* time. "but I just happened to see a mob of lady

111

truck drivers when I pulled up. And I mean they were all beautiful as hell, but they aren't even close to the woman that hopped out this green truck."

Evelyn found herself blushing. "She a bad bitch ain't she?"

"Next!" the older Hispanic cashier yelled.

Eve and the *unknown* stranger moved up. She set all the drinks she had on the counter for the cashier to ring them up.

"Well, I'm not a fan of referring to a woman as a bitch," he told her. "Unless one *is* a bitch; but, the woman I am speakin' of is for sure drop dead gorgeous." He extended his hand out to her and introduced himself. "I'm Prince; it's nice to meet you, beautiful."

"Honey are you gonna pay me or what?" the cashier hollered out to Evelyn ignorantly.

Evelyn whipped her head around to the lady and snapped. "¡Puta! ¡Callate la *maldita* boca antes que tumbe los *putos* dientes!" she threatened, shocking the shit out of the woman.

She turned back around to see a surprised look on Prince's face.

"My name is Evelyn, but everyone calls me Eve."

Prince was still stuck. "Forgive my ignorance, but you speak Spanish?"

"Yes. I'm Dominican; Taino-Arawak all day, every day, papi."

"Eeee, *joooeee*, lil' mama bad *and* she Spanish!" Prince exclaimed with a big goofy grin as Evelyn paid for her things with her debit card.

"I'm Latina," she then corrected, as she always did when someone called her Spanish, Hispanic, or, *Latino*, as if she was a *man*, and not a *woman*. "Spanish people are from Spain. My family is from the Latina America A.K.A the Caribbean."

"Oh, damn. My fault, Eve. Well, it is very nice to meet such a beautiful woman. Uh... what are the chances that I might can get yo' number, so I can maybe give you a call some times? I would love it if I could take you out to dinner," Prince said. "And I happen to be goin' up to Waukegan to help out my cousin that can't stay out of trouble."

Evelyn's iPhone rang just then. She pulled it out of her butt pocket and saw that it was Gloria. She ignored the call and tucked it into the pocket of her little denim Givenchy jacket.

"We might be able to do that, but I'ma have to let you know off the rip, I am a very busy woman."

She got her purchases bagged up and stepped off to the side while Prince requested a couple packs of Newport 100s and a couple of packs of grape White Owls.

"I dig it, lil' mama," Prince replied as he pulled out a wad of big faces from his pocket, stunting a little for the beautiful dominicana. "I'm a very busy man, too, you dig? I'm got a few businesses that are doin' *real* good, which is why I'm pissed that I gotta go rescue this dumbass nigga before he gets himself killed."

"You're from Chicago aren't you?" Evelyn guesses, hearing how he talked, very familiar with how those from Chiraq spoke, since many of the drivers at her brother's company spoke the same way.

"Yes, ma'am. I'm from out *Willy*," Prince said, paying for his items. "I be on Central Park and Arthington, you feel me? It's a real *Ghost* town over there," he added, with a sly smirk.

Evelyn chuckled. "Okay. Well, I…"

Her phone ringing again made Evelyn halt mid-sentence. She groaned and pulled her phone back out. It was Gloria again. This time she answered the call.

"¡Mamahuevo! ¿¡Que carajo quieres?!" Evelyn snapped.

Gloria snapped right back. "¡Puta! ¡Vamos! ¿¡Que 'stas hacienda?!"

"None of yo' motherfuckin' business, goddammit! Fall the fuck back y *mamate* un bicho!"

Evelyn ended the call on her and looked at Prince, who was laughing his ass off.

"What the hell did you just say? Besides the part that you said in English?" he asked her.

"I told my employee to wait," Evelyn capped, putting what she had said, very mildly.

Prince chuckled again, stepping to the side so the customers behind him could handle their business. He was about to speak when suddenly, the door to the store flew open, and in marched a thick-ass chick with an auburn-colored spiral curled Afro. She looked furious.

"¡Mamahuevo!" the girl snapped, stomping right up to where Evelyn stood and getting right in her face. "¡Te lo prometo, sit u me dices que me mame un bicho ever fucking again, on my *momma*, bitch, me voy a romper la *puta* cara!"

Evelyn waved her off as Prince found himself wondering what the milk-chocolate beauty had just said in Spanish.

"Bitch, tu no quieres problemas conmigo. I will beat cho' muthafucka ass in front of 'erybody. Ahora let's go," Evelyn said, grabbing the girl's hand and ushering her towards the door.

Right before she left out, Prince saw Evelyn look back at him. She gave him the flirtatious smile ever. He smiled back, then she was gone.

That is the baddest bitch I dun' ever seen in my life, and she a muhfuckin' gangsta, joe! On the Five, I gots to get at her... oh shit! I ain't get her number!" he thought, panicking to himself.

Prince hurried out of the store and ran to the rear of the building, just in time to see the two semi-trucks pulling off. He saw the big Volvo that Evelyn was driving and quickly put the phone number that was on the sleeper wall under the D.O.T and the Motor Carrier numbers, all under *Dedicated Transport, LLC* into his phone, praying to the Man above that it was *her* number.

He saved it into his phone and glanced up when he heard a squealing sound come from Evelyn's truck. His eyebrows furrowed up when he saw a piglet's head just above the bottom of her window line.

Wow, she had a pig, now that is different, he thought to himself, liking her more and more every second.

CHAPTER 12
JAVI

"*Mmmm*, Javi, baby, you so damn nasty!" Michelle giggled as she stood bent over the bed, in Javi's sleep, with her dress up, thong to the side, and Javi's face between her booty cheeks, tongue licking all up and down her ass crack.

BBBBBBBBBBBBBBB!

"*¡Ay, shit!*" she then screamed out, when Javi motor-boated booty hole. "¡Diablos, Javier! ¡Tu 'ta *fucking* loco!"

Javi's laughter was muffled in her crack. He continued teasing her, making her head spin around like she was on a merry-go-round of pleasure and bliss. A minute later he lowered his face and started sucking on her pussy. Michelle squealed, rising up on her tippy-toes, eyes squeezed closed, hands clenching the blanket on the bed, burying her face down in the bed as her man's amazing pussy-eating skills made her feel lightheaded.

Parked inside of *PJ&D Industries*, Javi couldn't resist getting in a quick one while waiting to get loaded with his family's most valuable product. Demon and Diamond were outside, running around with Pablo as ChaCha threw around a thick rope chew toy rope that she had brought out of her truck to entertain her dog while she waited for her load as well.

The minute Javi saw opportunity, he wasted no time in getting his woman into the sleeper and closing the privacy curtain to block out any prying eyes. Michelle already knew what he was on and she was on the same thing.

Pretty Ricky's *Juicy* featuring Static Major bumped, fueling Javi's freak mode as he got his woman hotter and hotter for him.

"Fuuuuuck, Javier! I'm 'bout to cum!" Michelle announced, feeling it coming on very strong.

Javi then motor-boated the pussy. Michelle cried out and blasted him in the face with her hot sweet juices.

"Goddammit, yo!" she shouted, feeling like her knees would give out if she tried to stand upright. "On everything I love, wait 'til we get home, man!"

Javi stood himself up, laughing at her, then gave her ass a smack.

"Yo' ass ain't gon' do shit but tap out *again*, punk," he shit-talked, then smacked her ass once more.

Michelle stood up and gave him the middle finger. Javi leaned in and kissed her lips, then as he slipped his tongue into her mouth, he fixed her thong and her dress for her.

"Tap out ain't even in my vocabulary, boo-boo," she told him, when he pulled back.

"And yet, you just said it."

Michelle punched him in his chest. She winced as pain shot up her arm when it felt like she had just punched a wall.

"You might wanna use padded gloves if you gon' keep tryna punch a hard-body nigga like me, bae."

"Oh really?" Michelle quickly dropped down, grabbed him by his legs and lifted him up so that he fell backwards onto the bed, then she jumped on top of him, grabbed his wrists and held him down. "Now what? Pop that hot shit now, nigga!"

Javi burst out laughing at his woman. "You must really think you did somethin', huh?"

"I bet you can't get up, though."

Javi tried to boot her up off him. But she had him. He tried to wiggle from under her, buck her off him, then he tried to kick out from under her. It was no use; his woman was trained in keeping someone where she wanted.

Michelle busted out laughing then. Javi took advantage of her momentary lapse in keeping her guard up and flipped her off him. Then he rolled on top of her and pinned *her* under him.

"Yeah, muthafucka! What! *Ha!*" he teased, using his body weight to hold her down.

Michelle looked up at him with a sly smile. "Come here, baby."

Javi shook his head.

"Nigga, if I tell you again, I'ma head butt you, yo," she threatened.

Javi obeyed her. He leaned down as she lifted her head up. She licked his lips, tracing them with her tongue. Javi started kissing her. Michelle wrapped her legs around him and started grinding her pussy against his crotch. She was already yearning for some more loving, but she knew they didn't have time to get it in again.

"You bogus as hell, Michelle," said Javi, as broke their kiss.

Michelle busted out laughing at him. "How am *I* bogus, Javi?"

"'Cause, nigga, yo' ass tryna make me drive this muhfucka wit' a truckload of fuckin' coke in the trailer with a hard-ass dick! Asshole!"

Michelle screamed laughing at how screw-faced he was.

"What is so funny about that?" he asked, now twisting his lips up at her.

"Your f-*bbbbbb... hey!*"

Right before she could say the word face, Javi ran his hand over her lips, stopping her like he had did when they were still in their teens. He laughed his ass off at her, so hard that tears filled his eyes. Michelle reached up and muffed his face.

"¡Mamao!" she called him then.

KNOCK! KNOCK!

They both were interrupted by the sound of knocking on the sleeper.

"Hey, bunny rabbits!" they heard ChaCha holler just outside of the truck.

"Hold on! We naked!" Javi shouted back, making Michelle giggle.

"No, you are not. I can see you, asshole!"

Javi and Michelle turned their heads and saw out of the sleeper window, ChaCha's face up against it, looking right in at them. She smiled and waved at them when they realized the jig was up.

"Okay. We're coming," Javi said to her.

"You're already loaded. Pull up and I'll close your doors for you, then we're out," ChaCha told him.

She went and opened the driver's door of Javi's truck. Demon and Diamond jumped up inside and ran into the sleeper, both jumping up onto the bed as Javi and Michelle got up. Michelle rubbed her wildly excited dogs down while Javi got into the driver's seat to pull his Large Car up from the loading dock.

***

XAVIER

Arriving in St. Louis, Xavier made his way to where the construction company told him to take their $400,000 machine. Hopping off the highway, he came to the massive site that had two big mobile trailer offices, both displaying the company's name on their sides. Amongst them, a dealership's worth of other expensive machines were parked in three rows.

Xavier pulled in and parked, putting his log onto *On-Duty/Not-Driving: Unloading*. Neveah was fast asleep in the sleeper. Kenzie decided to let her be, since Precious was there to watch over her.

She and Xavier got out of the truck and within forty minutes, had the excavator unloaded and parked with the other machines. The company's supervisor came out of one of the offices to inspect the dirt-digger, then signed the paperwork Xavier presented to him. Xavier quickly took a picture of the signed Bill of Landing then he emailed it to Javi so *he* could forward to the factoring agent.

Neveah had woken up while they were getting the excavator unloaded. Xavier got Precious out while Kenzie got her daughter out. Deciding to go for a walk so Precious could use the bathroom and stretch her legs, Xavier and Kenzie took the little one and the dog out along the perimeter of the construction company's field to enjoy a little down time, before getting back on the road.

Walking side by side with Xavier, holding Neveah's hand, Kenzie sighed to herself. The mid-day warmth, the sun, and the freedom she felt from her abusive baby daddy had her feeling so safe and happy. What mattered more to her, was that her daughter was safe, and Neveah seemed genuinely happy around Xavier.

Kenzie's mind then went to how *she* herself felt around Xavier. He gave her butterflies, every time he looked at her with those deep brown eyes and gave her that million-dollar smile. His deep, smooth voice gave her a hot and fuzzy feeling that she couldn't remember any other man ever making her feel. There were so many different words and feelings bouncing around in her head, she was amazed that it could all exist in such a short amount of time.

Xavier felt an attraction to the voluptuous red head that he never thought a woman could make him feel. For the longest part of his adult life women, to *him*, had been like interchangeable parts to a machine. He never allowed himself to let feelings get attached, but Kenzie and her daughter had somehow planted themselves deep inside of his mind, and in his heart.

His mind went to the Chicago Bulls jersey she had on that allowed her tattooed arms to show. The red leggings she wore had her shapely lower half looking so damn good, and the red, black, and white Retro Air Jordan 5s she had on her feet displayed her sporty swagger. Xavier loved it when women wore Mikes, even more than when they wore high heels.

Kenzie had dressed her daughter the same as her. It made Xavier smile; like mother, like daughter, and one thing her always appreciated, was when a woman was a good mother to their child.

Trying hard to keep the moment pure and not glance at Kenzie's fat juicy derrière again, Xavier pulled out his phone and called his brother.

"Dimelo que paso, my nigga," Javi answered, sounding like he had just won the lottery.

Xavier chuckled. "Fuck wrong wit' chu', bro? Soundin' all geeked up 'n shit."

"Ain't shit wrong with me, nigga. I'm happy; can't you tell?"

"Yeah. Yo' ass must be at it again with Ms. Washington Heights."

He heard Javi bust out laughing.

"I was just callin' to check on you and my future sis-in-law, though. Y'all good?" asked Xavier.

"Yep. We Gucci, bro; escortin' ol' St. Nick 'round Chi-Town for an early visit, ya dig I'm sayin'?"

"Yes siir. Me y las mujeres down here in the Lou, takin' a lil' stroll with Precious before we head back."

"Meet us at the Skillet," Javi suggested then. "I bet money Kenzie and Neveah will *love* it there."

"That sounds like a plan, bro. Bet it up. You talked to Eve?"

"I just got off the horn with her. She and Gloria wit' Payton and Olivia out in Naperville right now, pickin' up more cars to take to Libertyville; they should be back around before you and the ladies get back. They finna meet up with us, too."

"Aight cool. I'll put a little pep in my step and get back asap. Cuidate, 'mano."

"Ya tu sabe," Javi replied.

Xavier ended the call and got Kenzie's attention. "My brother suggested we all meet up at this restaurant up in Racine. You tryna go eat the best food on the road?"

Kenzie nodded her head right away. "Hell yes. I am starving, and I know my baby is, too."

"Well let's get back to the truck and head back," Xavier told her.

He then scooped Neveah up into his arms. She screamed in delight as he flew her above him like she was a plane, running towards the truck with Precious running right alongside them. Kenzie smiled her ass off as she followed, hoping that there wouldn't be an end to Xavier being a part of their lives ever.

***

JAVI

Around nine that night, Javi and ChaCha delivered the last of their multi-million dollar loads to one of Danny's massive storage facilities out in O'Hare. Just after ten, they both parted ways from Jamaica and the Rastas. They headed back to Joliet while Javi and ChaCha headed north to get to Wisconsin.

"Yo cheatin' ass man!" Javi shouted into his CB's mike as ChaCha blew the doors of his Kenworth off, passing him like he wasn't doing 75 miles an hour.

Michelle laughed at how salty he looked. She knew that Javi hated losing, but he should've known better than to think that he could hang with ChaCha. Michelle didn't know much about trucks, but she knew that out of all the money ChaCha had dropped into her truck to make her rare X-edition Peterbilt one of the dopest big rigs on the road, that a good portion of it went into beefing her engine up. The high-performance Pittsburgh Power-upgraded twin-turbocharged Caterpillar C15 engine under the hood was insanely powerful. It put down 1,200 horsepower to the ground, nearly double the power that Javi's ISX Cummins engine had. ChaCha's Pete made Corvette and Mustang lovers think they were in go-karts when they thought they could beat her in a race.

"You mad?" came ChaCha's voice, taunting Javi. "Well get madder, then, lil' nigga! Deuces!" she then shouted.

Javi and Michelle watched as flames shot up out of her big 10" Dynaflex exhaust stacks. As if she had just hit the NOS button, ChaCha took off like a rocket, yanking her empty trailer along with her as she easily broke 100 miles an hour.

"Goooooddamn!" Michelle's eyes went wide in shock, jaw damn near in her lap.

Javi shook his head. "I need a faster engine," he said to himself, salty as hell that he kept getting left in the dirt by *La Diabla*.

CHAPTER 13
JAVI

The-Dream's *"I LUV YOU GIRL"* remix, with Young Jeezy pounded as Javi cruised at the speed limit. He entered Racine County a quarter after eleven at night. Michelle moved her body to the beat, turnt up, signing along with the chorus. Diamond sat next to her seat, while Demon was laid out on the floor in the sleeper.

ChaCha had completely disappeared, but her voice hadn't. She had still been talking shit over the CB, teasing Javi, until she had gone out of range.

Leaning back in his chair, Javi kept one hand on the steering wheel. He saw the exit sign for Exit 333 of Sturtevant coming up. Already in the granny-lane, Javi put his right turn signal on and prepared to get off the interstate. A little less than a mile ahead, he could see the lights and the sign to the Iron Skillet up on the left side, along with the big sign for truck parking at the Petro Lube truck maintenance and repair business next to the Skillet.

Javi had been looking at the signs for a few seconds, then put his eyes back to the windshield, when suddenly, Michelle screamed.

"Javi, watch out!"

He hurried to look to the right and saw a semi-truck running up on his right, riding on the shoulder of the highway. It passed him with haste. Javi peeped that on the driver's door of the rig, the company's name... *Fast Lane Logistics.*

Michelle saw it too. It then swerved in front of Javi and immediately started slowing down.

"¡Mamahuevo!" he snapped, hitting his brakes to avoid slamming into the back of the rig's trailer.

Javi had been going too fast too slow down enough to avoid a collision. He yanked the steering wheel to the left, jumping over to the middle lane, just narrowly missing catching the rear end of the Fast Lane truck's trailer, and in doing so, Javi missed the exit to get off at Highway 20.

Diamond started growling, as if she could sense trouble in the air. Demon got up and went to her side, sensing the same. Michelle was suddenly hit with a bad feeling in her gut. She held on to the door and her seat as Javi grabbed his mike and started snapping on the driver of the rig.

"Aye, what the fuck is yo problem, pendejo! Si you outta yo mind?!"

Javi and Michelle then heard an evil laugh come from the CB.

"¡Estas muerto, *pinche* dominicano! ¡Estas muerto!"
WHAM!

A hard bump from behind nearly made Javi lose control of his truck. He and Michelle were almost thrown from their seats. The dogs slid forward and collided with each other.

Javi held onto the steering wheel, keeping control of his truck. He looked in his mirror and saw another rig was behind him. Another quick glance to his left, and as he passed by the Perto Lube, he was able to see ChaCha's Peterbilt already parked in the big truck parking lot in between the diesel repair business and the Iron Skillet.

"Dammit!" Javi cursed, as the rig behind him rammed him again, just as he came up on alongside the rig that had cut him off.

Michelle could see the silhouette of the driver behind the wheel as they sped side by side, pushing *waaaay* past the speed limit, shooting over the overpass that ran right over Highway 20. She had just been able to catch a glimpse of his teeth, as he smiled sinisterly at her.

"Oh, you think it's sweet, bitchass nigga?!" she yelled out of her window, reaching for her handbag up on the dashboard. "I got somethin' for ya' bitchass to cheese at!"

WHAM!

The driver swerved hard to his left and smacked into Javi's truck. Diamond and Demon flew to the side, Demon hitting the shifter and knocking it out of gear.

"Motherfucker!" Javi cursed, hurrying to put the shifter back in gear and hitting the gas.

The driver swerved into him again, then again, causing significant damage to Javi's prized W900L.

"Haahaa! ¡Te due, puta madre!" the driver yelled out of his open window to Javi. "I'm gonna kill you both, bitch!"

Michelle got her automatic Glock 18 out of her bag and cocked it, taking aim at the driver's face.

"Kill these nuts, paisa!" she shouted back.

"¡Hijole!" he shouted in panic and hit his brakes.

But due to brake lag in a semi's air brake system, the brakes didn't come on fast enough.

BRRRRRRRRRRRRRRRRRR!

"Smile at that bitch!" Michelle shouted when his face blew off.

The rig veered to the right, careening off the highway onto the shoulder. The trailer caught an edge and slid inwards, bring the tractor with it. In seconds, it was flipping and tumbling until it was just pieces in the grass.

The truck behind him rammed Javi again, then from the CB, he and Michelle heard, "That was my brother, pinche puto!"

Javi grabbed his mike and shouted back, "Fuck you brother and fuck you too, mamahuevo!"

Javi then told Michelle to hold on. She did her best to grab a hold of Diamond and Demon. Javi glanced in his mirror and saw the rig gaining on him to ram him again.

Barely any traffic was out. Javi was grateful for that. There would be less of a mess to be left behind if things got worse.

Come on, pussy! Bring yo' bitchass on! he thought to himself, waiting for the right second to make his move.

The Fast Lane rig sped up again. Javi timed it just right. As soon as the truck was close enough, Javi smashed down his brake pedal and made the rig slam into him harder than the driver meant to hit him.

"Yeah! Ha! What, Bitch!" Javi shouted in triumph, letting back up off the brake pedal, his trailer wheels rolling freely again, leaving the disabled Fast Lane truck behind.

Michelle screamed out with excitement when she saw in her mirror, the rig's front end so badly damaged, that it could no longer pursue them.

Just then, a call from ChaCha came in, making the music cut off. Javi quickly hit the Bluetooth button on the head unit, answering the call.

"Yo, Javi, where y'all at, son? I know I ain't dip on y'all like that, yo," ChaCha said, with a chuckle.

"What happened was, that punk-bitch hijo de la gran puta sent two of his trucks at me!" Javi told her, fuming as he pushed 90 miles an hour. "Them fuckin' paisas rammed the fuck outta my truck, cuz!"

"What?" shouted ChaCha in disbelief. *"Where are you?"*

"A few miles out from Caledonia!"

"Uh… Javi!" he heard Michelle say just then.

He glanced over at Michelle just then, seeing her pointing out of the windshield to something that was ahead of them. Javi looked out the windshield himself and saw what she saw.

***

CHACHA

"Javi! ¡¿Que 'sta pasando, papacito?! ¡Hablame!" ChaCha pleaded as she high-tailed it out of the Iron Skillet, back to where she had parked her truck, panicking with fear when Javi told her that Victor Gomez had sent killers in trucks at him and Michelle.

With her Bluetooth earpiece paired to her iPhone, as she made it to the filled parking area, she could hear Michelle, in a terror-stricken tone of voice, call Javi's name. Then she heard Javi curse.

"Javi, come on! Fucking talk to me man! What the hell is going on?" ChaCha shouted, right as she made it to her extensively customized X-edition Peterbilt.

"There's some shooters up on this overpass that I'm comin' up on, cuz….and there's a bunch of red beams dancin' around in my cab," Javi finally spoke.

"¡Coño!" ChaCha cursed. She yanked her suicide-style driver door open, jumped up into the cab where Pablo was anxiously awaiting her on the bed of her luxurious flat-topped style sleeper berth, already sensing that something was wrong. "I'm on the way, Javi! I'm coming!" she told him, punching in both knobs on the dash to release the tractor's and the trailer'ss brakes and slamming the shifter into gear.

She shot up out of her spot, whipping it to the left when her trailer cleared from the rig that was parked on her right side.

Just as she hurried out to get towards the exit, ChaCha grabbed the mike to her CB and frantically called out to Xavier, and Evelyn.

"Yo, what up, cuz? You cool?" came Xavier's voice.

"No! Get on my back door! Now! ¡Vamos!!" ChaCha demanded, nearing the exit to the access road.

"¿Que pasa?" came Evelyn's voice just as ChaCha whipped nearly eighty feet of tractor-trailer out of the lot and onto the main strip like it was a Camaro.

"Victor fucking Gomez happened! Get your ass in gear and come onnnn!" ChaCha shouted.

She raced to the light where the Iron Skillet sat at the corner where the little road met with Highway 20. Ignoring the red light, ChaCha hurried and banged such a hard right turn onto 20 that she nearly tipped her truck over, all the while cutting off a few east bound cars.

Her phone was still on, connected to Javi's. She was listening to him and Michelle. She could hear Demon and Diamond whimpering and barking.

"Oh fuck," she heard Javi say as she hurried under the I-94 overpass, reaching the other side in seconds.

She got to the light at the other side and whipped another truck-tipping left turn. ChaCha gasped when she started hearing assault rifle gun fire.

"Bae! Get down!" she heard Javi yell to Michelle.

"*OhmyGod, ohmyGod, ohmyGooood!*" ChaCha panicked, tears filling her eyes as she raced up the on-ramp to get on Javi's trail.

She banged gears on her 18-speed transmission, faster than she had ever done before. She begged her truck to go faster, though she was already doing 55 miles an hour in just seconds of entering the highway.

ChaCha's truck blew flames up out of the massive exhaust stacks as she hammered north to find Javi and Michelle. On the passenger's seat, Pablo sat, looking out of the windshield, as if *he* was looking for them, too.

Then, ChaCha heard tires screeching, mixed with some many gun shots. A loud crash followed, along with ear-piercing scraping sounds that nearly blew ChaCha's ear drums.

"JAVI! JAAVII!" she shouted, not knowing what the hell just happened, doing more than one hundred miles an hour now.

Javi didn't answer. All she could hear was the *rat tat tat tat* of bullets hitting what she was sure was Javi's truck.

"Javi! Micheellee! *Pleeaassee! Talk to me!"* ChaCha cried

"Bae? Michele? Hey, Michelle? Bae! Fuck! Micheellee! Bae, wake up! Please baby, wake up!"

ChaCha gasped, tears falling down her face, as she started fearing the worse from the way Javi was crying, and the way the dogs were whimpering, the way dogs did when their humans were hurt... or worse.

TIPPIN THE SCALES 2 | DIESEL

CHAPTER 14
JAVI

"Michelle! ¡Amor!" Javi cried, trying to shake his fiancée back to a conscious state, crying his eyes out from the sight of blood gushing out of the gaping wound in the right side of her forehead. "Please baby, not like this! *Come on! ¡Abre tus ojos! Please!*"

Whimpering at his side, Demon and Diamond stood, sharing Javi's anguish as he tried to wake the beautiful brown dominicana.

Inside the cab, between it and the big spacious Rolls-Royce Phantom-luxurious sleeper berth, Javi was kneeled over next to his future wife. She was laid out on the driver's side of the wall of the truck. Loving his future-wife way more than a material possession, Javi decided it was best to sacrifice his half million dollar show truck, rather than to lose his woman to the bullets flying into his cab from the Mexican sicarios perched up on an overpass that had been ahead of him.

He had slammed on his brakes and yanked his steering wheel to the right, to make his trailer jack-knife and slide to the left where *he* was, keeping the passenger's side, where his woman was seated, out of reach of the bullets. The truck then flipped and landed violently on its driver's side, scraping the road until it came to a stop a few hundred feet away from where it initially flipped.

The shooters continued firing, hitting the undercarriage of the truck, which had little effect on any of them getting inside the truck where Javi, Michelle, and their dogs were now trapped

Javi begged and pleaded for his woman to wake up. She didn't move an inch. Blood continued gushing from her head wound. The shooters kept on dumping, refusing to give up until they knew that they had accomplished their mission.

BRRRRRRRRRRRR! BRRRRRRRRRRRR!

The shooters were relentless, blasting in a firing line from above, down at their target. Javi crept low to the sleeper and hurried to get a shirt out of one of the drawers he kept clean clothes for long over-the-road trips. He hurried to press the shirt down on Michelle's head, to hopefully stop, or at least slow the bleeding. Holding it there, he knew he couldn't let go, even to go get the H&K G36 he had tucked in the custom-made gun rack under the sleeper's bed. He could only hope and pray that ChaCha would get there, and soon.

***

DIABLO

"Go! Go! Go! ¡Avansan! ¡Avansan!" commanded Diablo, the leader of the Mexican hit squad that were shooting tactical AR-15s down at the flipped over semi from up on the overpass a hundred feet in front of him. "¡Apurnese antes que los pinches policia llegen, cabrones!"

Sitting back just before the overpass started in his big black Chevy 3500 dually pick-up truck, the sicario boss yelled orders to his team of thirty highly trained soldiers, all of whom were ex-military from Mexico, just as he was, through the 2-Way radio that was linked to the earpieces in all their ears.

Sitting in the passenger's seat next to Diablo was his second-in-command, a huge mountain of a guy that went by the nickname Botas. Like Diablo, Botas was older and had deep brown skin, signifying the deeply rooted Aztec background of their descendants. Botas was large and round with tattoos all over his clean-shaven head, whereas Diablo was a little taller than average, in very good shape for a guy that was in his early 50s, had long black hair pulled back into a ponytail, and he had a hard face with a scar from the left eyebrow, down to his cheek.

Diablo was called the devil by many, all around Mexico. He was said to be pure evil in the flesh. He had acquired the fearsome reputation during his time when he was in the Mexican Special Forces, then he ended up joining a para-military group. Soon after, he over-threw the top dog of the group and took over and quickly established a name for himself as a ruthless son of a bitch that had no regard for human life, if the price was right to eliminate it.

He had been given a mission by Victor Gomez: Kill Javier Valdez, and anyone that got in his way.

The job would earn Diablo a hefty half a million dollars, which had gone up from pennies, since nobody had ever gotten close to successfully getting the young rich cocaine trafficking Dominican.

Diablo and Botas watched their crew as they all got their rappelling gear from the motorcade of black Hummer H1s and prepared to drop down onto the highway and finish the job. Not a single one of them cared that traffic was still flowing from the southbound lanes, while it began backing up on the northbound side, due to the over-turned 18-wheeler.

Just as the first group hurled themselves over the concrete barrier, Botas started shouting with panic, pointing out of his window.

"Diablo! *Mira!* Look!" he urged, seeing what was speeding up the highway towards the scene.

Diablo looked and saw the red semi-truck coming, flames shooting up out of the exhaust stacks. Not too far behind it, they both saw a bunch more big rigs coming. Diablo cursed. He knew it was the rich Dominican's people coming to rescue him, like the drug-trafficking truck-driving mafia they were known to be.

¡Maldita sea!" Diablo cursed.

Knowing that when help arrived, he would likely only have half of his crew left… or none at all.

The sounds of tires screeching came. He saw the red truck's brakes had slammed on and the trailer jack-knifed as the driver hurried to bring it to an abrupt stop. They were both close enough to see that it was the queen of the Valdez family's multi-billion-dollar empire get out of the truck with a big dog, and a huge military-grade gun that she had to hold with both hands, and right as the others from his crew launched themselves over the side of the overpass to join the others.

***

XAVIER

Xavier followed ChaCha around the traffic jam that was building up a short distance back from the flipped over truck blocking the middle of the road ahead. She braked and skidded her truck and trailer sideways, then jumped out with Pablo and her big-ass street sweeper. Xavier did the same. He grabbed his M4 Carbine that had been altered into a fully automatic spitter, fitted with a 120-round drum.

"Go back to the sleeper and stay down!" the muscular younger brother of Javier Valdez told Kenzie, then he jumped out of his truck, closing the door behind him to keep his all-white beast inside the truck to keep watch over the ladies while he helped ChaCha.

BRRRRRRRRRRRRRRRRRRRRRRRRRRRRRRRRRRRRRRRR RRRRRRRRRRRRR!

As ChaCha blew her big M249 SAW at the shooters, all taking cover by the tall overpass's concrete pillars, Xavier raised his gun and started dumping at the ones that were rappelling over the side from up top.

He hit two of them with ease. They dropped from nearly fifty feet in the air and hit the southbound side of 94, splattering all over the three lanes.

The other three made it down and scattered, taking cover like the others that were finding it very difficult to get a shot off with such a big gun fitted with a 200-round ammunition box being blown at them by one hell of an angry Latina.

Shots flew at them from a different direction, hitting a few of the cars that had been abandoned by innocent by-standers that had high-tailed it away from the highway shoot out in sheer fear.

Xavier crouched down by a minivan; ChaCha dropped down behind a pick-up truck and started shooting from under it, pointing at where she saw dark figures moving.

Pissed as shit now, Xavier jumped back up and started walking out into the open, not caring about the bullets that were flying at him.

"¡Mamahuevos, come on! Let's go,!" he shouted at them. "Y'all pussy muthafuckas want my brother? Holla at me first!"

He opened fire again, sweeping left and right at everywhere he had seen movement.

***

EVELYN

Coming to a skidding stop, Evelyn jumped out of her big Volvo 780 with her fully automatic Heckler & Koch G36, keeping her baby miniature pet piglet inside of the cab. Right behind Evelyn's rig, her girlfriend Gloria jumped out of her Kenworth T660 with her own G36. Behind Gloria's rig,

Payton and Olivia jumped out of their identical 10-car transporter Peterbilt 388s, with AK-47s. The two ran to catch up with their boss and her lover and got to it, as if shoot outs on the highway was a common thing for them.

***

CHACHA

She popped another one, hitting the sicario right in the center of his chest. His body armor did nothing to stop the barrage of bullets that hit him up like a ball of angry killer bees. A gigantic hole opened in his chest, putting his guts right on the asphalt.

She crept low and made it to the space between the front of Javi's trailer, and the back of his truck's sleeper. She yelled out over the shooting, just as Pablo came to her side with a bloody hand clutched in his teeth. He dropped it on the ground and licked his chops clean of the blood of the man he had mauled to death.

"Javi! Michelleee! Can y'all hear me?"

***

JAVI

Javi heard ChaCha's shouting for them from somewhere outside of his truck. He had long ago heard the shooting start, but had been clueless as to when someone would come help him get Michelle out of there before she bled to death.

"Baby! They're here! They came for us!" he told his still-unconscious fiancée, while keeping the blood-soaked shirt pressed on her head.

Despite her still being out of it, Javi did discover that she was breathing, but she was in serious need of medical treatment… *fast!*

"Javier?"

"Yeah, I can hear you, cuz!" Javi shouted up through the smashed passenger's side window. "Michelle's hurt, she's bleeding, and she won't wake up!"

"Okay… just hold on! I'm gonna get y'all outta there!" ChaCha swore to him.

***

EVELYN

Evelyn, Gloria, Payton, Olivia and Xavier stood tall against the remaining sicarios. They stood side by side and dumped on them fearlessly while traffic on the southbound side started building due to a few cars up front peeping gun fire and skidding to a stop, blocking the highway and getting out to run away.

Seeing ChaCha dart out from the space between her brother's trailer and his tractor, with her dog hot on her trail, Evelyn provided her with cover, running to where the tractor was and making sure nobody could get the drop on her.

ChaCha had started trying to kick in the windshield. Evelyn heard tires screeching as the glass broke. She looked up and caught sight of a big black pick-up truck taking off from one side of the overpass.

Gritting her teeth, Evelyn raised her G36 up, pointing at the pick-up and wrapping her finger around it. Then Gloria stepped up to join her, then Payton, Olivia, and Xavier.

***

DIABLO

"Haaa! Na nan naa boo boo! You stupid pendejos!" shouted Diablo as he floored his 3500 along the overpass, him and Botas laughing at how not a single bullet penetrated the truck, nor did a single one even come close to shattering a window. "It's bullet proof, muthafuckas! Ka kow!"

Botas was laughing so hard that his eyes filled with tears. Bullets hit off the reinforced glass, literally inches away from his head.

Diablo rocketed across the bridge to the other side, escaping the pointless gunfire. He knew for a fact that his crew was gone, but he could always get more. He always did.

"We'll get 'em next time, Botas!" he shouted over the loud hum of his diesel engine. "They haven't heard the last of us, carnal!"

"¡*Orale, guey*!" Botas shouted then, already anxious to make the come back and put the Dominicans in the dirt, once and for all.

CHAPTER 15
JAVI

He held onto his fiancée as ChaCha kicked the windshield in. When she made a way out, Javi carefully carried his woman out of the destroyed truck with Demon and Diamond right behind them.

"Come on, come on! We gotta go!" ChaCha said urgently, peeping the massive traffic jam in both directions. "My people at the state trooper station gave us just fifteen minutes to get you before they have no choice but to swoop in and get everyone!" she said, hearing sirens from afar.

From down the northbound side of the highway, Javi could see so many red and blue lights that it looked like an entire police force was on the way.

He ran behind ChaCha and Pablo to where her X-edition Peterbilt was. When she opened the suicide-style driver's door for him, Javi carefully climbed up inside and carried Michelle into ChaCha's sleeper, with all three of the dogs right behind, as fast as he could. He laid her on the bed then and pleaded for her to hold on.

He heard ChaCha closed the door, then the sound of her releasing the air brakes came. The truck lurched forward after she slammed it into gear and dipped off.

Please, man! Don't take her from me! Please! I need my woman! I ain't shit without her, man! Javi thought, talking to the Man above with his silent thoughts.

He leaned over and kissed his woman's forehead, then held her hands as ChaCha sped her ass off, shooting northbound to get as far away from the bloody massacre as she could, as fast as she could.

***

XAVIER

"Y'all okay?" Xavier asked the gorgeous red-head that was tucked low in his Kenworth's flat-top sleeper, holding onto her terrified 4-year-old daughter, while Precious sat at their side, doing her job of keeping her eyes on them.

"Y-Yeah… we're good," Kenzie replied, slightly shaken by the craziness that had just taken place a few hundred feet away from her and her daughter. "What happened with Javi and Michelle?" she then asked, hoping that the two were okay.

"Javi's good, but Michelle's hurt bad, ma. She a soldier, though. Sis been though worse; she'll pull through," he assured Kenzie, knowing exactly all the things Michelle had been through.

Kenzie got her and her daughter up from the sleeper floor as Xavier speed-shifted gears to keep up with ChaCha's insanely powerful and fast Peterbilt.

"Just so you know, though, Kenzie," Xavier said as they flew past the mass of abandoned vehicles on the southbound side of 94. "Things are gonna get real rough. If you want me to get you and lil' mama a plane ticket to wherever, I can do that, but a whole bunch of them punk bitchass cartels niggas is gon' die. We finna get on some gangsta shit wit' all they asses, ma."

Kenzie looked over at him as he kept one hand on the steering wheel, while one was on the shifter. Xavier glanced over at her after he spoke what he had to say, then looked back out the windshield.

Neveah, who was holding onto her mother, had grown so attached to Xavier in the short time that she and her mother had been in his life, and him in theirs. Kenzie had grown attached as well and couldn't fathom leaving.

"I won't leave you, Xavier," she told him then. "I am here to stay; *we* are here to stay, if you'll have us."

A smile broke out on his face. He couldn't help it. He had a feeling that Kenzie would refuse to leave. Now, he had even more of a reason to handle the bullshit with his family, so that he could make it back to Kenzie, and Neveah. He found true joy when he was around them. It was different than what he felt when he was with Nena, or his other chicks. Being around Kenzie, it felt easy to him. He didn't want that to end any time soon.

***

EVELYN

Following her brother and ChaCha off I-94 at 4 Mile Road in Caledonia, Evelyn's eyes filled with tears as it all hit her like a bag of bricks. Her big brother was a target for a man that had managed to get the drop on her, inside a busy gas station, and was likely only alive because ChaCha had happened to pop up and save her ass.

Thinking about how close Javi and Michelle had come so close to losing their lives had her livid. She was tired of it. She was beyond ready to see this Victor Gomez guy die. Death had already taken her great uncle Pedro, and her big cousin Tommy. She couldn't handle losing anyone else.

"These bitchass paisas wanna keep fuckin' with my family?" she said angrily to herself, ignoring her piglet nudging her thigh with his snout. "Aight, then! I'm finna get on some straight G shit now, joe. On *God*, nigga!"

A little more than thirty minutes later, the Valdez posse made it back to Javi's truck yard. Most of his trucks were gone as usual. ChaCha parked her Pete at the first garage bay door.

Xavier skidded his Kenworth to a stop behind hers and quickly jumped out to go help, while Evelyn and her ladies all parked their trucks and hopped out as well.

As the suicide passenger's door to ChaCha's Pete opened, Xavier ran up to help Javi as he was about to climb down with her in his arms still. He handed Michelle to Xavier and got down behind him, with ChaCha and the dogs all jumping out as well. Evelyn hurried to open the garage. They all hurried inside to with everyone worried sick about Michelle.

****

MICHELLE

Her eyes opened to bright light shining through the narrow slits. Immediately, she felt her head start to throb. She closed them again. She felt like there was a competition subwoofer pounding right inside of her skull. Then, a bit of relief came when she felt something cold and wet on the side of her head. She took a deep breath, filling her lungs, but couldn't manage to open her eyes yet. Everything hurt; she couldn't remember anything. She wondered if it was the light of heaven trying to get through her eyelids, at least until she heard the smooth sound of her fiancé's voice.

"¿Amor? Baby? Can you hear me?" she heard him ask, from somewhere very close to her.

Then she felt a wet tongue lick her left arm, while a nose nudged her right leg. She heard two different whimpers and knew her dogs were at her sides, along with her man.

Michelle tried to speak, but it came out as more of a groan. She nodded her head, but even doing something as simple as that hurt her. Her brain felt like it had broken loose, and any which way she moved her head, it rolled and crashed into her inner skull.

"Bae, hold your head back so you can drink," she heard Javi say to her.

She did as he said. Tipping her head back, she parted her lips. She felt the rim of a cup touch her lips, then she tasted a cool fruity liquid that instantly helped. When she had drank it all, Michelle cleared her throat, then she again tried to open her eyes.

When they focused in, Michelle saw everyone was there. She recognized Javi's office right away. Javi was in front of her; Demon and Diamond were at her sides. Xavier, ChaCha, Pablo, standing next to ChaCha, Evelyn with her piglet, and Gloria, were all behind Javi; behind them, she saw Payton, Olivia, Kenzie, and Neveah.

Demon and Diamond both nudged Michelle's side again. They could sense her pain and sought to comfort her.

"What happened?" Michelle asked, finding her voice was no longer hoarse.

Javi sighed, feeling horrible. "I had to roll us, bae. To keep them bitchass fucktards' bullets from gettin' you," he told her, which immediately jogged her memory of when the shooters on the overpass started shooting, hitting the truck as Javi continued speeding towards it, and what Javi had ended up doing to keep her from being shot.

His extreme measures to protect her, which not only included putting himself in the line of fire but sacrificing his one-of-a-kind $425,000 custom Kenworth that Michelle knew Javi dearly, made her smile through her pain. She knew that Javi would literally do anything to protect her, but the constant reminders made her feel so good and cherished.

"Did y'all get 'em?" Michelle then asked him, just as Xavier brought her a bottle of water, and some aspirin.

Javi nodded his head. Just as Michelle took the pills and washed them down, a dark-skinned woman with a low-style haircut, wearing bright colored scrubs and Crocs on her feet entered the office, carrying a medical bag.

Right away, the nurse got to work. She unwrapped Michelle's head, uncovering the gash at the right side of her forehead. She cleaned it, then numbed it, before stitching the skin together.

Javi held her hand the whole time. He was livid that his girl was the one bleeding, and not him.

"Baby, I am so sorry. I swear on my uncle Pedro, yo, I'm finna turn *up* on that bitchass nigga Victor! On *God* I am!"

"Papi, tu no tienes na' de qué disculparte," Michelle told him as the nurse finished by putting a water-proof bandage over the stitches, "it's those pussy muthafuckas that's gon' be sorry, yo," she added, now with a murderous look in her eyes that made Javi start grinning like the Grinch.

Everyone in the room saw Michelle's eyes and felt the temperature in the room drop a little. ChaCha was a real live gangstress; Evelyn and Gloria were both beasts. Javi and Xavier were businessmen but, when need be, they were with the shit, but Michelle… she was a certified killer. It was purely suicide to screw with her people, her man, or *her*. Period.

Javi leaned over her and planted a soft kiss on her lips. He smiled lovingly at her, admiring how strong she was.

"I love you, baby," he told her then.

"I love you, too, guapo," Michelle replied, smiling up at him.

"I'ma step out for a second and let the nurse get you back together." Javi kissed her forehead. "Be right back in, okay?"

She nodded, then watched him leave out of the office. Xavier hugged her and kissed her forehead, then ChaCha and Pablo did, and Evelyn. She watched them all head out as well, leaving Kenzie, her daughter, Payton, Olivia, Demon, and Diamond inside with her, along with the nurse.

***

JAVI

144

"She's so strong," he said, just as his eyes started watering up.

Xavier, Evelyn, ChaCha, and Pablo, were all in front of him, sharing Javi's pain. Then, in a sudden fit of rage, Javi spun and put his fist through the wall.

ChaCha gasped. "¡Dios mio! ¡Javi, ya!" She went and threw her arms around him before he could go completely berserk.

Javi screamed out at the tops of his lungs, then, he broke down and cried his eyes out. She held onto him while he shook like he was possessed by a demon. Xavier and Evelyn both stayed silent, eyes welling with tears, both were as angry as Javi was. Evelyn ran to hug her oldest brother with ChaCha then, unable to help it. "It's okay, papacito. We're all here with you; let it out," ChaCha then told him.

The walk-in door to the garage opened and they all looked and saw the two wild-ass puertorriqueñas step in, followed by the up-and-coming fashion designer. Behind the three beautiful ladies were the seven members of the *Steel City Mafia*.

Yessinia, the caramel-complexioned Nuyorican, was said to be the Bronx-born goonstress twin of the famous actress Gina Rodriguez. She stood a statuesque five-foot-nine and was stacked with the body of an urban magazine model, with long silky black hair that fell to her plump rear end. She was more than just a street chick, though. Currently, she was a 1st Lieutenant in the military, a straight boss chick in fatigues that was well on her way to commanding her own unit. And with her, was her sister from another mother.

Her best friend that she had been tight with since the 6th grade, Gabriella, whom everyone called G-Baby, a.k.a. The Gangsta Boo was a ride or die chick by the very definition of the term. She was a Chicago-born goon, straight out of Humboldt Park. She stood an inch shorter than her home girl, had long dark and luscious hair, and had skin that was the same color as pancake syrup. Also, like Yessy, G-Baby was thick as hell like a K.O.D dancer. In the military with Yessy, the same unit, G-Baby was a 2nd, Lieutenant.

Felicia, their high-yellow home girl was from Pittsburgh, PA. She was the girlfriend of the youngest Steel City Mafia goon. At five-feet-seven inches tall, with a body that was a little more than petite, but not exactly thick, with long dark hair that was tinted with blue and in stylish braids. When she wasn't on goon shit with her man, the beautiful gangstress was busily putting together new ideas for the up and coming clothing and accessory line she had been dreaming of creating since she was a kid.

The wild card of the Valdez family, Macho, his older and much bigger dread-head brother Tool, both of them massively built pretty-boy gangster type dudes, were joined by their SCM brothers Perry, along with Perry's three cousins City, City's younger twin brothers Cee and Dee, and, the 1st and only Lady of the Steel City Mafia, Lacey, an Italian beauty with long silky jet-black hair that everyone swore was the clone of *JWoww*, the crazy beautiful and sassy *Jersey Shore* alum, but Lacey had *way* more ass, breasts, and was *way* taller.

CHAPTER 16
CHACHA

She got so excited when the goon squad came in. With whom was already there, the New York, Chiraq, and Steel City gangsters were the icing on the cake. Walking up to her, Javi, Xavier, and Evelyn, the 6'3" Macho, golden-brown skinned with long cornrows in his head that reached down to his massively wide chest, tattooed like Wiz Khalifa, was like a taller bulkier version of Javi. Many mistaked *them* for being brothers instead of cousins, but while Javi's eyes were green, Macho's eyes were a bluish gray.

Right with him was 6'6" brother, who was built like an oak tree, and tatted up to the max. He was often joked to be like the Dominerican version of Waka Flocka Flame.

Right behind the two was Perry, 6'5" of light brown skinned beast, rocking a bald fade, his 6'1" cousin City, the 6'2" twins, and the statuesque 5'10" Lacey, all of them ready to show Illinois how Pittsburgh gangsters regulated.

"I am beyond tired of this bitchass nigga's shit, yo!" ChaCha said to the ten goons, plus Javi, his brother, and his sister. "I was *very* serious about letting this fucking *idiota* have his little fun, *trying* to stop us, but now, I am *very* serious about how painfully his death needs to be!"

Heads nodded; no words were spoken.

"I'm ready, prima," Javi was the first to say, looking at her with blood-shot red demon eyes. "¡Te lo juro por Dios! I'ma kill *all* them pussy muhfuckas, joe! On *God*!"

"Naw, yo. I want you here, papa. Michelle needs her man at her side."

Javi *sooo* badly wanted to protest, but he knew ChaCha was right.

Evelyn stepped in front of her big brother then. "Don't worry, bro. We got it. We finna-"

"Ah! *No!*" ChaCha interrupted, cutting Evelyn clean off, pulling her back away from Javi and spinning her to make her face her. "You are *not* getting into this, Eve. *On* my mama, B!"

"But… Ximena!" Evelyn whined, calling ChaCha by her government name.

"But *nothing* Evelyn!" ChaCha exploded, stepping her 6', voluptuous, tattooed, butter-pecan-brown frame to just inches away from the super thick 5'7", golden-brown skinned Evelyn, glaring down into Evelyn's eyes with *angry* frosty Arctic Blue eyes. "*Diesel*," she continued, calling the king of the Valdez family by the nickname she had chosen for him back when she and Danny Valdez were just teenagers. "Would break out of prison and fucking kill me if I let you get involved in all the blood shed that is about to happen. Not to mention Ricardo and Rosie!" she said, adding Evelyn, Xavier, and Javi's father and mother into the equation. "¡Asi que! Read my lips… *You are not going*!"

Right before Evelyn could burst into tears from being denied the right to ride for her big brother and Michelle, Xavier and Javi both stepped up to her.

"Just chill, sis," Javi told her, as Evelyn's eyes welled up with tears. "Michelle might need a lil' girl talk at some point, and she loves yo' wild ass to death."

"I promise you, though, Eve," Xavier then chimed in. "I will make sure to save you a lil' ass to kick," he promised her.

But that wasn't enough for Evelyn. She wanted some heads to roll *now*, after she chopped them off with her machete. It took everything in her to hold her tongue, but somehow, she found the restraint to hold back.

"Okay. Well. I still gotta go deliver the cars I got on my truck," she then told them, plotting her own course of action inside of her head.

The door opened again and in came the Commander-In-Chief of the Valdez family's army of Caribbean goons, followed by his right hands, all of them straight out of Kingston's treacherous *Tivoli Gardens* garrison.

The tall slim and light-skinned Jamaica, as everyone called the O.G., had been in the trenches with Javi, Xavier, and Evelyn's grandfather Deigo and Diego's brothers Juanito and the deceased Pedro since the three ol' heads had begun building their family's notorious multi-billion-dollar empire, all off of the purest cocaine to eve come out of the Dominican Republic. The dread head was a gangster Bob Marley, who always kept a machete and AN AK close by. Even in his mid-50s, the Rastafarian goon boss was still handling business and getting his hands bloody like age wasn't nothing but a number.

Behind the 56-year-old was his captain, Gold Mouth, a man as black as tar with the shiniest gold teeth one would ever see. With Gold Mouth was Shabba, Mango, Face, and Kingston. They were all under Gold Mouth and had their own crews twenty fearless and loyal Rastas. Not only were they protectors of the family, but they were all members of Tivoli Gardens' feared *Shower Posse* mob, and they did *not* play well with others.

***

JAVI

"Nephew," Jamaica said, with a strong accent, embracing Javi like the nephew he had been to him since he was born, "me glad 'ya are okay, and me glad 'dat Michelle is okay. Me and me shottaz are hea', and we gonna 'andle 'dis, 'ya 'ear me, tiguere?"

Javi nodded his head. "Thank you, tio."

"Seguro, 'mon." Jamaica turned and looked at ChaCha then. "What 'appened 'ta 'dat 'beetch 'ya had workin' 'de bomba-clot fuckboy, Ximena?" he asked her, clearly upset about all that she had told him.

"Ask me that the next time you see me," she replied darkly, having plans to go feed her dog bitch-meat.

Jamaica's anger dissipated a little. He chuckled, knowing that the blue-eyed New York goonstress had something totally evil in her head.

"Send me 'de locations 'ta all 'de Rojas-Gomez spots, and me destroy *all* 'ah 'dem," was the last thing the head honcho said, before he and his soldiers headed out to get to work.

After they were gone, ChaCha hugged Javi and Evelyn, then she led the others out to go get to it themselves. Javi and his sister stayed where they were, watching their family head towards the exit. ChaCha whistled loudly and outran Pablo, right to her and followed her out of the garage.

Seconds later, Javi and Evelyn heard multiple engines start up, then tires screeching, then there was silence.

Javi looked at his sister. He saw her trying to hide a smirk. He shook his head. He knew his baby sister too well.

"Cuidate, Eve," he told her, then he made his way back to enter his office and be with his woman.

Inside, he saw the American-born Jamaican chick Payton, and Olivia, a marvelously beautiful Japanese-Sicilian mixed woman, comforting Michelle, along with Evelyn's auburn-afro-wearing cocoa-skinned girlfriend Gloria, Kenzie and Neveah. Demon and Diamond were still at Michelle's side. The nurse was just finishing up patching the dominicana up.

"She's gonna be fine, Javier, as long as she gets some rest," the nurse said. "and I mean *rest*, young man… not that craziness you two can't take a break from."

Javi laughed. "Sheeeeeit, you talkin' to the *wrong* one about *that*, Mrs. Green."

"Stop tellin' on me, Javier," Michelle threw in.

They all laughed.

"You are all in my prayers. Call me anytime you all need me. Hopefully next time, though, it'll be to invite me to another one of those big cook outs y'all are always throwin'," Nurse Green said with a warm smile.

Grabbing her medical bag, she headed out, leaving a positive vibe behind like she always did.

Gloria, Payton, Olivia, and Evelyn, all hugged and kissed Michelle on her forehead, then they hugged Javi. He noticed they all ignored Kenzie, but didn't say anything about it.

The ladies left out and went back to their trucks.

Javi stayed at his woman's side. She smiled up at him, reaching a hand up and stroking his beard. She saw how exhausted he looked, but more than that, she could see how terrified he had been.

He smiled back at his brown-sugar-complexioned beauty. Javi loved his woman so much. From the day he met the 5'5" belle in Manhattan, New York's famous Washington Heights neighborhood, where she was born, raised, and turned into a killer, he had been head over heels in love with her. Now, at 26-years of age, Michelle was a seasoned veteran in the *rid-the-world-of-miscreants* game.

Javi then turned his head and looked at the statuesque Kenzie. She was standing a few feet away, holding her daughter in her arms.

She looks just like ol' girl on 'Wild 'N Out', he thought to himself.

"You two okay?" Javi asked her, realizing that it was the first time he had met them in person.

Kenzie nodded her head. Neveah hugged her mother tighter, still a little scared and timid at the same time.

"We're sort of used to craziness, with my whack-ass baby daddy 'n all," she told him.

"You ain't ever gotta worry about him again, ma," Michelle told her. "I'm sure Xavier informed you that dude and his mans are sleepin' with the fish."

Kenzie did remember. After a horrible beating Stacks, the father of her daughter, where he had thrown her through the glass patio door of her apartment, Kenzie had met Xavier by chance, in the lobby of her building, when she was packing up to flee Illinois. She was bruised, the scars and scratches were still on her arms and on her face. She'd been scared to death. Xaveir rescued her, and following him bringing both her, and Neveah into his home, Javi and Michelle eliminated the woman-beater and his homie Rambo.

"He did. Thank you; both of you," Kenzie said, meaning it from the bottom of her heart, though she really wished it didn't have to come to Stacks dying.

Michelle saw Neveah looking at her. She waved and smiled.

"Hi pretty, little girl. My name's Michelle, and Xavier is my bro. What's your name?"

Neveah warmed up to Michelle right away. "Neveah Cardoza."

"Wow. That name is so beautiful, just like you!" Michelle cooed. "Don't be sad anymore, okay? You wanna' get some ice cream?"

Neveah's smile grew big. She nodded her head rapidly.

Javi assisted Michelle as she rose up from the chair.

"Okay. Come with me and we'll go find some in the kitchen."

Kenzie set her little girl down on her feet and let Michelle take her by her hand. Demon and Diamond followed the two as they left out. Javi smiled at them, then he looked at Kenzie.

She looked at him, slightly timid herself.

"My brother almost never connects with women like he's did with you. Can you do me a favor, Kenzie?"

"Yes."

"I'm not sure what you did to make my bro rock wit' you the way he does, but whatever you did, keep on with it. Bro needs a good woman in his life that won't drive him nuts."

Kenzie chuckled. "Um. I can only be how I am, Javi."

"Do that and keep doin' that. Now let's go see what type of ice cream my lady and Neveah found," he told her.

Javi led the way out. Kenzie followed. They walked in silence to the kitchen, where they found Michelle and Kenzie pulling out tubs of chocolate chip cookie dough ice cream.

***

EVELYN

How the fuck they gon' tell me to chill?! I'm a muthafuckin' tiguerasa! The pussy muhfuckas almost killed my brother and Michelle! Fuck fallin' back, joe! I'm finna get on some G-shit!

Evelyn fumed, barely able to concentrate on keeping her loaded auto-hauler in the granny lane. With her multi-million-dollar load of exotic automobiles in her ridiculously expensive NASCAR-style enclosed luxury car-carrier, Evelyn sped her ass off to hurry and get to Mundelein, to deliver them and take her truck to the back to the yard and get her some revenge for the attempt on Javi's and Michelle's lives.

Behind her, Gloria kept the same pace in her exotic car transporter. Behind her, Payton and Olivia, and their armed motorcade of Rastas, every single one of them with their gas pedals to the floor.

A$AP Ferg's *New Level* featuring Future pounded from the custom sound-system in the tall and spacious Shaquille-

153

O'Neal-sized sleeper berth in Evelyn's Volvo 780. She gripped the steering wheel tightly in her left hand while her right hand rested on the shifter to the truck's 13-speed transmission.

As she continued thinking about the situation she finally came up with an idea. It was enough to make her smile in a way that could scare a demon. Typing on the touch screen as fast as he fingers would allow, she found the person she was looking for and hit dial.

"Wha'gwan?", answered Shabba. "Every 'ting okay up 'dea, Evie?"

He and his crew were right behind Olivia, in black H2 Hummers, thumped up with military-grade firepower that Jamaica had decreed for them to use to shoot first, fuck asking questions at *any* time, if anyone got too close to any one of the ladies.

"I need your help, Shabba," Evelyn told him.

"Gon' 'n kick it 'ta me, gyal," the dread replied.

Evelyn told him her idea. Shabba shot it down right away.

"Ya know me can let cha' do 'dat, Evie. Ya' brudda' would 'ave me head."

Evelyn sucked her teeth. "I knooow you ain't scared of Javi, man. You're like, twice his size."

"Nah, nah, nah, little momma. Evie. Don't do 'dat; me a *real* rude bwoi, 'ya ear me? *Strrraight* out Tivoli Gardens! Me gets *wild* wit' 'de guns 'n 'de knives!"

"I mean… I *hear* you, Shabba, but hearin' and seein' ain;t the same. Javi and Michelle almost *died*, unc! How you really expect me to *not* ride for them?"

Evelyn then heard Shabba speak in a language that she couldn't understand. A minute later, he was back to her.

"Okay, Evie. Whaddya 'ave in mind?"

She almost screamed with excitement. She told him what she wanted to do. To her surprise, Shabba was very impressed by it.

154

"Me like 'dat, gyal! A'right! Let's do it!" he told her, geeked himself.

Evelyn ended the call with a giant smile. Ready to turn up on everyone involved in Victor Gomez's organization, she turned up her music and got right in mode when she heard Twista & The SpeedKnot Mobstaz' "*WARM EMBRACE*" was on.

"Eeeeeee, joe!" she shouted, then started rapping along with the old gangster anthem. "*I looove the element of surprise of takin' these hoes' lives, wit' my customized Fo-Five, got enough ammunition to knock of you, yo' crew and some mo' guys! You muthafuckas betta' get wise!*"

CHAPTER 17
XXXX

Marcello gritted his teeth, eyes squeezed closed, gripping the hips of the curvy Salvadorian chick that he was fucking hard and fast from the back. Her face was buried in the blanket on his bed. Her screams of bliss were muffled by it and the Reggaetón music that bumped from the sound-system in his bedroom.

"¡Aaayyy, Marceellooooo! Yeeess! Fuck me, papi! Oooo, yeah, papi! Give it to me!"

Marcello went harder on her, hitting it even faster. He reached up and grabbed her hair with his left hand, pulling her head up. He smacked her ass repeatedly with his right. He held onto her long, luscious mane and put his back into it, fucking her so good that she wanted to scream out that she loved him.

Both were high off a mixture of cocaine and molly. They had been fucking each other's brains out since Marcello had bumped her at the club that his crew had thrown him a surprise b-day bash for his 29th birthday. They had brought forth the big-breasted Latina; she had been paid handsomely to suck and fuck him all night long.

Marcello let her hair go a minute later and made her put her face back down and toot her ass up again. He pulled his dick out of her soaking wet pussy, parted her ass cheeks and before he entered her back door, he spit a wad of saliva onto her puckered asshole.

"Oooooo… ssssss!" She bit her bottom lip as she felt the tip of his cock entering her ass.

Just as he started stroking her, the doorbell rang. He ignored it and kept on trying to get his nut. But the doorbell kept on ringing, pissing him off.

"Man, what the fuck, joe?!" he snapped.

He yanked his dick out of her. She immediately started cursing him out as he hurried to put his boxers on.

"Marcello, what the fuck, dude?!" she snapped.

"Shut the fuck up Carla, damn!" he shot back at her, hurrying to get his basketball leisure shorts on. "I'll be right back! Just shut up and stay here!"

Before Marcello stomped out of his bedroom, he grabbed his Mac 10 from the underwear drawer and cocked it, chambering a 9mm round. Cursing up a storm as the doorbell continuously rang, he got to the front door of his lavish home. He hit the light switch on the side to turn the porch lights on and then he looked out of the peephole in the door.

Standing outside of the door, Marcello saw a tall woman in a Domino's Pizza uniform, holding a pizza carrier case.

"Maaaan, what the fuck?!" Marcello said to himself, as he hurried and unlocked all the heavy-duty locks and snatched the door open. "Bitch!" he snapped at the woman, who was much taller than him. "It's two o-clock in the fuckin' morning! Fuck is you doin' at my door tryna deliver a pizza?!"

The girl smirked at him. Despite her amazingly beautiful face, the look in her cold Arctic Blue eyes made him catch chills up his spine.

"I'm not deliverin' pizza, *mamabicho*," she said to him, grinning evilly. "I'm delivering a message to your boss."

Faster than his eyes could even follow, the girl snatched out a .45 Desert Eagle from inside the pizza carrier case and pointed it right at his face.

"OH SHIT!" he panicked

Jumping a step back, Marcello went to raise his Mac up at her and pop her ass, when a fist came flying from his right and crashed right into his jaw, ringing his bell.

The blow rocked Marcello so hard that he spun around in a circle, his gun flying out of his hand, then he fell to the hardwood floor, with double vision.

Marcello's head rang like the bell of Notre Dame. He groaned in pain, trying to focus his eyes on the dark figure that was now looming over him. All he could see was the silhouette of a very big guy, wearing all black, but he heard growling from somewhere very close to him.

"Special delivery, bitch," the man said to Marcello, as the girl in the Domino's uniform stepped into the house, and closed the door behind her, locking it.

***

XAVIER

Standing over Marcello, Xavier looked down at the main money runner for Victor Gomez's cartel. The guy writhed in pain; ChaCha stood at the door, with her big cannon in her hand.

"Who… are you?" Marcello asked.

Xavier smirked at him. "The man with a hungry dog."

He saw Marcello crane his neck, then his eyes went wide when he saw Precious, and Pablo, sitting side by side at *his* side, both staring at Marcello like he was a big steak.

"Oh sh-sh-shhhiiiiit! Aye, man, what do y'all want?!"

"I want you to run all that cash that we know you got here," ChaCha stepped in and told him.

"And all the money you have access to that's in the electronic accounts, you gon' wire it to a different account, my man," Xavier told him. "Do that, and I won't kill you. That's word."

158

Xavier could see the color of Marcello's face go pale.

"He'll kill me, man!" he cried.

"What the fuck you think our dogs gon' do if you don't, pendejo?" ChaCha asked him.

"O-O-Okay… b-but y'all gotta help me get outta town afterwards, joe! For real, man!"

"Marcello!"

Xavier and ChaCha both looked at the tip of the hallway that led to the bedrooms and the bathroom. They saw the chick that Marcello had been digging out since they arrived come around the bend.

Marcello cursed when he heard his bitch's footsteps coming. Carla came around the corner and was about to curse him out, when she saw Xavier, ChaCha, Precious, and Pablo there, with Marcello on the ground, jaw swollen, looking like he was in deep shit.

Carla screamed.

BOOM!

ChaCha blew her head clean off with one precise shot to the dome.

Marcello didn't see it, but he heard her body hit the floor. Xavier grabbed Marcello and yanked him up off the floor, spinning him around so that he could see what had just happened to his bitch.

"You see that?! Huh, bitchass nigga?! You wanna leave this world without a head?!" he growled through clenched teeth.

"No, no! Okay! I'll do it!"

ChaCha and the dogs stood guard while Xavier forced Marcello to get his lap-top and wire the entire $95 million dollars that was stowed away in Victor Gomez's private business account to an account that would never be able to be traced by even the highest forms of the government, nor a brilliant hacker.

He then made Marcello take him to where he had boxes of cash down in a secured vault-like room in the basement.

He even forced him to carry each of the sixteen boxes out to the stolen GMC Jimmy that Xavier had peeled for the move.

"Okay! Y'all got the gwop, man! I need to get up outta here, 'cause I know Vic' is already gettin' notifications of the wire!" Marcello said, as Xavier took him back into the living room.

"Don't worry, fam," said Xavier. "We'll make sure dude's bitchass never finds you."

Then he and ChaCha gave their dogs the commands they had both been eagerly waiting for.

"¡Matalo!" Xavier shouted.

"¡Agarralo!" ChaCha shouted.

"*Nooooo!*" Marcello screamed, as the two killer Mastiffs pounced on him and started ripping at him like hungry wolves on a lone deer.

Xavier and ChaCha watched their dogs work. The viciousness of their attack made them both grin. Precious and Pablo ripped and yanked chunks of meat out of Marcello. He bled profusely from so many bites and rips.

Marcello begged for mercy. He could literally feel himself being eaten alive. Pablo then grabbed Marcello by his throat and chomped down hard on his Adam's apple. He bit down as hard as he could, crushing Marcello's windpipe. Marcello gasped for air, but Pablo refused to let go.

In less than half a minute, Marcello suffocated to death. Pablo then yanked as hard as he could and ripped Marcello's throat completely out. His body fell to the floor, blood pooling around it while Pablo chewed and swallowed the blood meat.

"Good booooy!" ChaCha praised him, patting her thigh to call him to her side.

Xavier called Precious to him and praised her as well.

"Aight, then. Meet you back at the yard, prima," he told ChaCha, ready to get to it.

"Yup. Cuidate, papa," ChaCha said, hugging him tightly.

160

They fled the house then. Xavier and Precious hopped into the old Jimmy; ChaCha hopped into her G63 AMG Mercedes truck with Pablo. They peeled off, heading in separate directions, with no intentions of returning to Javi and Michelle until they had painted Wauk-Town red.

***

XXXX

"Hey, ladies? I'm Andres, the owner of the place. What seems to be the problem here?" the owner of the popular Mexican restaurant, when he was brought forth by one of his waiters to a table with three stunningly beautiful women.

"Well, for starters, the food here *sucks*!" said the one with skin that was deep and brown like pancake syrup, with a femininely raspy voice.

"And secondly," chimed in the chick with the high-yellow skin tone, that was sitting next to her, "your boss has caused a lot of trouble, and since you work for him, *you* and this crappy-ass restaurant will suffer *because* of him."

Andres furrowed his brows. "I… I'm not sure I know what you're talking about, ma'am. I am the sole proprietor of this establishment."

Just then, the third woman, a caramel-skinned beautify that reminded him of a famous actress, of whom he could not remember the name of, due to the devilish look on her face that had him shitting bricks. She turned her head and looked at him with narrowed eyes. Andres took a cautious step back as she went to stand, with her hand behind her back.

"Wh-wh-what is this?" he asked, looking around at all his other customers, hoping someone would come to his aid, since his waiter had left him by himself.

"This is what it feels like right before you die, bitch," she said.

161

Just then, Andres heard screaming and yelling. He looked up and saw a mob outside of his restaurant. A few of them started throwing boulders at the windows and shattered them. Seconds after, they all ran inside with choppers in their hands, hoods and masked up. They immediately started shooting, targeting all the staff that worked for him.

Andres turned back to the girl and saw that both of her hands were in front of her now. In her right hand, she had a machete.

"Whoa, *wait*!" he pleaded as she winded up to swing.

BOOM!

Right before she could swing the sharp cutter and take his head off, a loud blast came followed by Andres' head exploding, put a damper in her plans.

Her jaw dropped as his headless corpse dropped. Right as blood poured from the stump, she saw the big muscular blue-gray-eyed gangster holding his .40 caliber Desert Eagle in his hand. Through the mouth hole of his ski-mask, she could see he was grinning at her.

"You fucking *asshole*, man! That was *my* kill!" she snapped at him.

***

THE STEEL CITY MAFIA

Mach busted out laughing as his brother, City, Cee, Dee, and Lacey put in work on all the restaurant's staff, while allowing the customers to flee.

"*Wooooo, 'ya almost had it! Ya gots to be quicker than that*!" Macho clowned his woman, imitating the words of an old man on an insurance commercial.

While Yessy contemplated rocking her man in his jaw for taking her kill, G-Baby and Felicia hopped up from the table. G-Baby peeped that one of the staff members had skipped past the SCM goons and was sneaking towards the entrance of the Rojas-Gomez-owned restaurant, which had been discovered to have a meth lab under it.

She took off to catch him. Felicia ran with her. They dove on him and took him to the ground. Yessy saw it and forgot about her man and his taunting smile.

She ran over to where her girls were and positioned herself over the guy as G-Baby and Felicia held him down on the ground.

"No, wait, please!!" the cartel cook begged.

Ignoring him, Yessy raised her machete up over her head, then with all her might, she brought the machete down, slicing nearly halfway through the top of his head.

He died instantly.

Yessy yanked the blade out and wiped his blood on the guy's apron. She turned to where her man still stood, trying hard to keep from laughing at her overzealous attempt to beat his record.

"Uh huh. Laugh if you want, mamao. I dare you, yo," the Nuyorican said to him.

"I'm good," he replied, trying so hard to keep it in. "How about we just make our way to the next one?" he then asked, as the last gun shots came, and all was quiet.

"Right," said Yessy, giving him narrowed eyes. "You and your crew better be safe, Antonio," she added, walking to him and getting herself a kiss.

"Soy un gangsta, my queen. I'm always safe," he replied, with a smile that made her want a quickie before getting back to work. "Y'all call us if you need us, though, amor, aight?"

"Baby, we gots this. Don't even trip. See you in a few," Yessy said, then she called her ladies, and headed out to the Excursion that had her Rottweiler, and Macho's Pit Bull inside, waiting for them.

"Antonio," Felicia said, walking up to him. "If you let ya' so-called sister, anywhere *near* my man, yo, it's *really* gon' be on when I get back. *Boyz*, cuz," she swore, like the Wilkinsburg Street chick she was.

Macho shook his head and watched her walk out of the bloody restaurant. Felicia hopped up into the Excursion and Yessy floored it, peeling off out of the lot.

Macho turned his head as his posse was coming from the kitchen area, Tool, Perry, City, Cee, Dee, and Lacey, all with steak tacos and burritos in their hands.

"These muhfuckas suck, cutty," Perry said, with a screw-face after taking a bite.

"Nasty-ass shit!" Lacey threw her burrito at the wall.

The others dropped theirs and headed towards the door to leave. Macho looked at his homeboy Perry, who was walking out with Lacey, right at his side. He snickered to himself, not even close to having any plans on stepping in between the two, even though Felicia was like as much a little sister to him, as Lacey was to him.

Sheeeeeeeeeeeit. Fuck all that. Bro a grown-ass man. If he dip and dab, then he dips and he dabs. He'll be aight with a black eye for a while, Macho thought, then he left out of the restaurant and joined his posse in the other Excursion, where the SCM dogs were in the back of the monster SUV.

CHAPTER 18
XXXX

An Hour Later

"Hey! What the hell are you doing?" Rodrigo Gomez yelled. He was the owner of *Lake Bluff Luxury and Exotic Auto* dealer ship, when he got calls from his security about four semis and a bunch of Hummers barging in and taking vehicles.

The man hurried out of his office, after trying to hurry up and wrap it up for the night. It was late, he was tired, and hungry. His wife was bitching about him being so late to get home every night, but he sold *way* more than just exotic super cars and foreign luxury vehicles.

When he got out to the big auto garage, of where he kept his most expensive and rare vehicles, he saw his four guards were being held at gun point by a mob of older men with dreadlocks.

At the rear of one semi-trailer, he saw his special edition Bugatti Veyron on the tailgate door, being lifted to the level of the top ramp, to be loaded into the luxury enclosed car-transport trailer, while a rare Porsche Carrera GT was being driven into the belly of the other luxury enclosed trailer. The other two semis were already loaded with Mercedes-Benzes, BMWs and Audis.

"Hey! What is this? Who are you?" Hugo shouted, looking at the gorgeous golden-brown skinned beauty with golden-blond hair and a shapely figure, working the tailgate of the trailer with the Bugatti on it.

WHACK!

"Aaagh!"

Hugo howled in pain when he felt the bite of a blade slice right through his right leg, severing it completely. He fell to the ground, his leg next to him, spewing blood from the stump like an illegally opened fire hydrant. Within seconds, the extreme loss of blood had him getting woozy and numb.

Before he blacked out, he peeped the golden-brown woman, now joined by a dark chick with spirally afro, standing next to him. The dark-skinned chick picked his severed leg up and waved it at him.

"*Psst!* Hey?"

Hugo looked up to where the sound of someone calling him was coming from. He saw a tall skinny man with dreads, holding the bloody machete that had subtracted a limb from him.

The guy grinned a demonic smile at him. "'Tank 'ya for 'de 'cahs, 'mon. We appreciate it. 'Dey'll look good wit' all me bruddas ridin' 'round in 'dem ova' in Jamaica and 'da D.R.," the dread said to him, "and, by 'de way... *fuck* 'de Rojas-Gomez cartel, muddafuckaz!"

He then raised the machete up high.

Hugo was too weak from blood loss to beg for his life. He closed his eyes and started praying.

***

SHABBA

CHOP!

"Woo! Dipset, bitch!!" Evelyn shouted when Shabba chopped the car dealership owner in the center of his face, silencing the younger money-laundering and Mexican meth and cocaine distributing cousin of Victor Gomez.

"Bomba-clot pussy-hole muddafuckas," Shabba grumbled, as he wiped the bloody chopper off on the owner's Armani suit jacket.

"I wonder if that hurt?" Gloria wondered.

"Who gives a fuck. Let's hurry up and get the rest of the cars," Evelyn said, wanting to stay on point and get up out of there as fast as possible.

While she and Gloria got back to loading their trailers, with the help of Payton and Olivia, a few of Shabba's men rolled out of the big garage with a humongous wooden crate on a pallet jack.

"Jackpot, Shabba! We found 'de stash and 'de cash!" said Power.

"Good. Burn 'de drugs and take 'cash and load it up to go to ChaCha's spot. It will go 'ta charity."

"Yah, mon," Power replied with a nod.

He left to hop to it. Shabba got his phone out and dialed his chief while turning back to watch over the ladies working to snatch the multi-million dollar loads of cars.

"Talk 'ta me, rude bwoi," Jamaica answered after two rings.

"Got 'de 'cahs, 'brudda, and 'de little mommas are safe,". Shabba informed the head honcho.

"Good. Maek sure 'dey get 'dere safely, Shabba; *No* fuck ups, 'ya ear me, rude bwoi?"

"Gotcha. Respect, brudda."

"Respect," Jamaica replied, then the call ended.

Shabba looked back down at the one-legged corpse. He started smirking at it.

"No worries, mon. Many of 'ya pussy-hole friends will be joinin' 'ya very soon. Learn from 'dat, bitch," he said, then he busted out laughing at himself.

***

XXXX

Out in Wheeling, Illinois

"Come on! Move it! Let's go! Pack up!" yelled Lucky, supervisor of the big produce packaging plant.

He yelled at his crew through the window of his elevated office. The window gave him a view of the massive work area below. He had one hundred and thirty workers there, all scrambling to pack up all the cocaine, heroin, ice, pills, cash, and guns that had been stored there for when other Rojas-Gomez distributors needed a quick re-up without having to wait for a whole shipment to come up from Tijuana.

Hundreds of millions of dollars' worth of illegal goods were kept there, shipped around Illinois and the surrounding states in *Fast Lane Logistics* trucks.

There were pallets with boxes of cash, all plastic-wrapped to be loaded into a few trailers that were backed to the loading docks, as were a few other trailers ready to be loaded with the drugs and the guns, to be taken to down to Mexico, until the heat died down. The plant was a crucial part of Victor Gomez's operation. Losing it would seriously cripple the cartel, to the point that it would struggle to get back.

Lucky saw his workers putting some pep in their step. He went back to his desk and grabbed the black leather briefcase that he had sitting on top. Unlocking it, he opened it up and was about to pull out the automatic AR-15 inside, when the phone on his desk rang.

He looked at the caller I.D. and saw it was the boss. Immediately, he picked it up and answered.

"¿Si, patron?"

"What's happening?! Are you all out of there yet?" Victor demanded to know.

"We're loading trucks as we speak, sir. We-"

A scream suddenly halted Luck mid-sentence.

"Hey? What the hell was that?" he heard Victor yell.

Lucky set the phone down, took his assault rifle out and ran back to the window to see what had happened. When he looked out of the window and saw what everyone was tripping about, Lucky's jaw dropped.

"Hijole chingada," he cursed to himself, shaking his head.

He went back to his desk, hearing Victor yelling for him to answer him.

"Lucky! Answer me, goddammit!"

"Boss. Everything is okay, sir. One of my guys… he got skunked."

"Skunked?! What the fuck does that mean, cabrón?!"

Lucky chuckled as the sight of the skunk running around the floor, after spraying a few of his workers replayed in his head. He told Victor what happened and busted out laughing.

"¡Pendejo! Stop fucking around and get my shit out there, *now*!" Victor exploded.

He ended the call without another word.

"Pinche culero, güey," Lucky muttered, hanging the phone back up.

BOOOM!

A powerful blast came the second he started chuckling at how scared his boss sounded. The explosion made the whole building shake. Screams of agony and cursing filled the plant then.

Lucky grabbed his AR, jumped up and ran to the window.

BOOOM! *BOOOM*! *BOOOM*!

Lucky's eyes went wide when he saw the little devices bouncing around on the ground in the mix of his fleeing workers exploding one by one. Each one sent hundreds of little pieces of fragmented metal flying in all directions. Shards of metal sliced through anyone too close to the frag-grenades when they went off.

His jaw dropped when he saw more than half of his crew drop. Blood, body parts, flew everywhere. The ones lucky enough to escape the grenades ran towards the emergency exit and pushed their way to freedom… until the sounds of machine gun fire outside stopped their hopes of living.

While the lucky ones high-tailed it out of there, Lucky's own privatized mob of mercenaries came running out from where they had all been gearing up to escort the high-value goods south.

"Find them!" Lucky shouted down to the tactical S.W.A.T team-like goons. "Kill them all!"

Forty men in total, all with AK-47s, wearing bullet-proof vests, headed towards the loading docks, where Lucky was pointing, knowing that the threat was right outside.

The two lead men got close to one of the doors and were flung high into the air when the door suddenly exploded, shattering into pieces.

The others were all pushed back from the blast, blinded by the fire and thick black smoke.

"What the fuck?!" Lucky blinked his eyes, trying to see through the smoke.

When it cleared enough, he swore that his eyes were playing tricks on him. But they weren't.

Through the smoke, the tail-end of a pick-up truck backed in. Mounted in the bed on a tripod, he was a big M60 machine gun, with a masked-up and hooded figure behind it.

The mercenaries all went to shoot at the figure, but the figure was faster.

BRRRRRRRRRRRRRRRRRRRRRRRRRRRRRRRRRRRRRR RRRRRRRRRRRRR!

The old school machine gun blew hundreds of 7.62mm rounds at the men, wetting them up as if they were caught in a torrential downpour. They all got soaked. Their body armor did nothing to deflect head shots.

"Motherfuckers! Okay! Okay! Let's do this shit!" Lucky growled through clenched teeth, then he raised his AR up, taking aim at the person shooting the M60, mowing his killers down as if it was the easiest thing in the world. "I see you, puto! Now you die!"

"Naw, yo. You die, bitch!" he heard someone behind him say.

Before he could even turn around-
WHACK!

***

G-BABY

His head hit the floor and rolled away. His body dropped to the floor, landing next to it. G-Baby held the bloody machete in her hands, smirking at the headless body.

"That's, what, twelve for me with the machete? I do believe I beat you," she said to Felicia, with a grin on her face.

With them, was ChaCha's younger cousin, Vanessa, who had joined them when Yessy scooped her up from her home, not too far from the plant.

"Whatever, Gabi," Felicia said, twisting her lips. "Let's just get done and go, smart-ass."

G-Baby went to the window and looked out. She saw Yessy in the pick-up's bed. Now at the sides of the pick-up, were six of the nine guys in Javi's crew.

O-Boy, Cadillac, and Bull were on the driver's side of the pick-up; on the passenger's side was JB, EZ Money, and Black. All six of them had Dracos with drums, gripped tightly, daring anyone to attempt to show up and help.

Felicia gave Yessy a thumb up, prompting her and the six truck-driving goons to get to the next phase.

G-Baby wiped her machete off on Lucky suit jacket. The phone on his desk started ringing right then.

The half-Puerto Rican, half Persian Vanessa went and picked the phone up, while G-Baby and Felicia stared ransacking the office, looking for what they had been told was there.

"Hello, can I help you?" Vanessa answered, like a pleasant secretary.

"Who the hell is this?" she heard a man demand to know.

171

"Hmmm... who do you want me to be?" she asked, toying with him.

"I want you to realize now, if you are not part of Lucky's crew, then you will die!"

"I guess this is the so-called prince of the Rojas-Gomez cartel, huh? Well, let me tell you something, bitch. Fuck you, fuck your daddy, and your momma, and everything you stand for. You fucked up trying to kill my people, and we are coming for you. We will not stop until you are dead. So, have a nice night, sir, and thank you for calling. Buh-bye now!"

Vanessa slammed the phone down and smiled smugly at G-Baby and Felicia, both looking at her like she was nuts.

"What? Stop looking at me like that and find it!" she told them.

They continued trying to locate it, but they came up empty. After five more minutes,

G-Baby went to the window and yelled out to Yessy.

"¡Trae la puta aqui!"

O-Boy went and grabbed the tied-up chick from the rear of the GMC Sierra's crew cab. Ignoring her cursing him out, he carried her up the stairs and entered the office, dropping her on the ground, inches away from where her dead husband's head was.

She screamed when she saw his dead face. Her bowels instantly loosened, and she shitted on herself, filling the office with a putrid odor that had them all wanting to get up out of there.

Felicia ran up and kicked the woman in her face. "You nasty bitch! Don't nobody got time to be smellin' that shit, yo! Now where the fuck is it?!"

The woman trembled with fear. "Y-You're just gonna' k-k-kill me when I t-t-tell you," Kelly wept.

WHAM!

Felicia kicked her in the face again, then she reached down and grabbed Kelly by her hair, yanking her head up.

"Last time! Where is it?!" Felicia yelled.

"In the top drawer of his desk! There's a false bottom!" Kelly screamed out.

G-Baby went and opened the drawer. Sure enough, there was indeed a false bottom. She pried it up and saw the flash drive there.

"Got it! Kill the bitch and let's go," she told the other two.

Kelly screamed, "Noo wait!"

Vanessa yanked her up, wrapped her arms around Kelly's neck and twisted as hard as she could, until they all heard the snap. Kelly's body went limp then.

Vanessa let her go. Kelly's body hit the floor, twitched, then went back limp.

G-Baby, Felicia, Vanessa, and O-Boy joined the others back down on the main floor. Yessy was just pulling out at cardboard box from the back of the pick-up, where her big Rottweiler and Red Nose Pit Bull were eagerly awaiting her.

Everyone hurried out as Yessy set the box in the center of the loading area. She ran to the pick-up and jumped into the bed. Bull mashed the gas and dipped up out of the building. Seconds later, the box full of C4 exploded with such a blast that it completely leveled the entire structure, and drastically shorted Victor Gomez's pockets.

And they weren't even close to being finished.

***

VICTOR

"¡Jefe! ¡Estamos listos!" yelled one of the sicarios, one of fifty, mobbed up and gathered in a large circle around the Rojas-Gomez cartel's shot caller. Each one of the hitmen had on all black with Teflon vests, artillery belts fitted with grenades and knives; they all had fully automatic AR-15s with 100-round drums, and back-up pistols. They looked like they could take on the Al Qaeda and the Taliban with ease "¡Vamos a matar *todos* de los pinches Valdezes!"

Victor stood above them, on the elevated loading dock of his massive truck terminal, out in the Lake County suburb, Zion, down a deeply recessed area on Shiloh Boulevard. It was late at night, dark, but somewhat lit up from the light poles around the property. He had enough illumination to see all off his hitters assembled and ready for battle.

Angry that Javier Valdez was still alive, and the two truckers he had sent to assist the so-called top-shot sicario leader had failed, Victor was now taking matters into his own hands. He had put word in that he needed ruthless killers. He was sent a gang of Mexican Mafia members that were eager to collect the astounding bounty he had put on the Dominican's head.

He stood before them in a custom Brioni suit. He was of average height and build. He wasn't really an intimidating man by looks, but he was connected, wealthy, and had no regards for human life.

"¡Caballeros!" he shouted out to them, getting their undivided attention. They all quieted down for the pretty-boy-type boss to talk. "These motherfuckers think it's a game! They think I am soft! That they can beat me!" he started with, looking at as many of them in the eyes that he could. "You! You are *all* killers! ¡Soldados! ¡*Sin* miedo!" he told them, "But you are all about to go at it with a very connected family! La *pinche* Valdez family has been a thorn in my side for years! It is time for them to take a trip to hell!"

A thunderous roar came from the mob as they cheered Victor on. But what he said next had them ready to race off and get on the business right then and there.

"I will give *one hundred thousand fucking dollars* to whoever kills the most Valdezes!" he told them all.

All the hitmen knew Victor's worth. He was a half-billion-dollar man, possibly even more.

"¡Orale, güey! ¡Vamanos, carnales!" shouted one of the men, eager to get that money.

"Let's get paid, vatos!" yelled another.

One man raised his AR up to the air and started shooting up, overly excited. The others all went silent abruptly. They all knew that the man's overzealousness had likely just pissed the money man off.

Victor glared at the guy, whom was in the front row. "¡Pinche *estupido*! The fucking police station is just up the fucking street!" he hissed at the man. "You're going to be the first person to die tonight, pendejo!"

"¡Jefe!" the man spoke back with a look of determination on his face. "I gonna kill *all* those pinche mierdas! They no can kill me!"

Victor then smirked at him. "But *I* can, stupid!" he told the guy, and as fast as a professional old western gun slinger, he whipped out the .357 Python revolver that was in his holster and thumbed the hammer back.

The hit-man's eyes went wide with shock. He screamed, "*No!*" right as the others all jumped away from him.

POW!

Half of his head exploded. His brains and blood flew onto those that were closest to him. His body dropped to the ground and a pool of blood poured out of his destroyed dome.

Victor looked at the others. They all stood silent. Even the few with the sticky crimson faces didn't move.

"Anybody else wanna make my place of business hot like a dumb fuck?" he asked them.

At the same time, they all shook their heads no.

"Great. Glad to hear it. Now… go! Go get those fucking Dominican bitches!"

Without words, they all took off running to where ten SUVs were parked side by side in a row. As they all started hopping into their vehicles, Victor began walking towards where his new Lamborghini Aventador Roadster was parked in front of his dispatch office taking his eyes off it for just a moment to grab the keys from his pocket.

BOOOM!

An explosion rocked the ground under him. Victor nearly jumped out of his skin. He turned and saw one of the SUVs had exploded, sending a giant ball of fire up into the dark sky.

The sicarios inside were instantly fried to death. Victors' eyes bugged wide with shock.

BOOOM!

Another one of the SUVs exploded.

Then four more of them blew up. Chaos ensued as twenty more of Victor's hired shooters were cooked to death in less than fifteen seconds. Those that remained hurried to hop out of the last few remaining Yukons and ran before they met fiery fates.

There was a moment of silence where they all breathed out, thinking they were safe.

BRRRRRRRRRRRRRRRRRRRRRRRRRRRRRRRRR!
BRRRRRRRRRRRRRRRRRRRRRRRRRRRRRRRRRRR!

Gun fire that sounded like thunder from a violent storm erupted just then. The very last of Victor's hitters flipped and flopped, limbs flying, bodies exploding as seven *Squad Automatic Weapons* chopped them up. In mere seconds, all that was left of them was bloody piles of meat, splattered all over the ground.

The shooting ceased then. The only sound was that of the fire that burned the SUVs, cooking the corpses inside of them. Victor raised up his gun, waving it around to dump at whoever he saw, for the first time in his life feeling genuine fear. But he didn't see anyone. He didn't hear anyone either.

He started back-pedaling then, pointing his pistol all around, looking for any movement as he got close to his Lamborghini.

BOOOM!

Less than ten feet away from his Aventador, the more than half-million-dollar car exploded, flying high up off the ground. Victor was knocked forward to the ground from the blast. He screamed when he saw the car was up in the air right over him. As fast as he could, he rolled and just missed being slashed to death.

He scooted away, terrified that he almost just got squashed by his own car. He looked at it for a second, then in a fit of rage, he screamed, "*Motherfuuucckkerr*!"

He dragged himself up off the ground, feeling pain everywhere. Holding his head, he looked around at the fiery carnage. He was miffed by it all.

"Whoever did this shit is dead! I swear to God, *you are fucking dead*!" he shouted.

The second he finished yelling his threat, the sounds of growling and barking got his attention. He whipped his head around towards the employee parking lot and saw a pack of dogs running in his direction.

"Ooohh fuuck!" he screamed.

He took off running, towards the tall chain-link perimeter closest to him, hauling ass from the seven vicious killers.

Three Pit Bulls and four German Rottweilers came running for him like he was food, and they were starving. Victor jumped on the fence and frantically climbed. The biggest of the Rottweilers jumped and missed his ankle by mere inches.

As if fire had been lit under his ass, Victor got up to the top of the fence. His foot slipped when he got to the top. He fell on the other side and hit the ground hard.

"Shit!" he cursed, feeling it in his back and the back of his head.

He heard the growling again. He looked to his right and saw all seven dogs were standing at the fence, glaring at him, gnarring their teeth, eyes locked on to him.

"F-Fuck you! Pinche bastards!" he said to them all.

"Yaa yaah"

"*Woo wooo*!"

"*Yeeeooo!*"

Victor heard shouting coming from behind the dogs. They all turned and ran away from the fence. When they had gone,

Victor saw seven figures, all of them in all black, hoods up, masked up, and holding some serious firepower.

Horror filled Victor as they walked in his direction, looking like a firing squad. When they raised their guns and pointed at him, advancing still while their dogs returned to them and trotted alongside with them, Victor pulled himself up and started running towards the old mechanic pick-up trucks parked just outside of his business, right as bullets began to fly in his direction.

***

THE STEEL CITY MAFIA

Macho, Tool, both armed with big automatic M249 SAWS, fitted with 200-round ammunition boxes filled with 5.56mm slugs held their powerful street sweepers as they advanced on the target, blasting at him as he dove behind a big Ford F550 service truck.

At their side, Lacey and Perry, sending swarms of 9mms at Victor Gomez with their MP5s.

City, Cee, and Dee, blew at Victor with their AR-15s, both equipped with M-203 grenade launchers, sent 300 Black Out rounds in his direction.

All seven of them lit the truck up, Swiss cheesing it to death.

They all competed; who was going to hit Victor Gomez and knock his shit back?

The Steel City Mafia goons continued blasting, relentless with it. Though he had disappeared from their line of sight, they were letting up until they heard him scream in pain.

Seconds later, the SCM boss, Tool, held up a fist, giving the order to cease fire. They stopped shooting, but kept their guns trained on the shot-up Ford, and their eyes right on it.

Macho's tiger-brindle female Old Family Red Nose Pit Bull, Dreams, stood at his side while Lacey's female Razor's

Edge blue nose Pit stood at hers. City's two big Rottweilers, Monster and Missy, were at his side; his twin brother Rottweilers, Benzo and Beemer, were at their sides and Perry's male reddish-brown tiger-striped, red nose Pit, Tiger, and Tiger's solid chocolate red-furred mate, Lady, stood obediently at Perry's side.

Nobody made a sound. They all waited as if they had all night.

Suddenly, Victor jumped and high-tailed it from where he had ducked from them at. They all opened fire again, following him as he ran for dear life. He just made it to the corner of his building and disappeared around it, escaping death once again.

"You luck bitch," Macho growled to himself, when they stopped shooting.

"Well get him, 'Tonio," Lacey told him, reassuring her big homie/ childhood best friend of it. "You know we will."

"Let's move, yo," Tool then commanded angrily. "Bitchass nigga wanna run like a hoe? Fuck it. We gon' make his ass anti up and come see us, right after we destroy *everything* his daddy built and gave to him, and his pee-on associates!"

"But first," Macho then said, as an evil smirk started forming.

He turned his SAW and pointed it in the direction of the six rows of Fast Lane semi-trucks that stretched ten trucks each.

Tool followed suit, then the others pointed at the eighty trailers on the other side of the tractors. They all squeezed and started dumping, destroying hundreds of thousands of dollars' worth of equipment with no hesitation.

Macho and Tool then turned their SAWs at the building and put so many holes in it that the roof collapsed.

All done wreaking havoc on Victor's spot, they all took off and ran back towards where they had two big early 2000s Ford Excursions on lift-kits with bulky off-road wheels sitting in the dark field across from the entrance the terminal. They got the dogs up inside the two monster SUVs, hopped in themselves, then behind the wheel of one, Tool mashed the gas and peeled off, witch City pushing the second one right behind him, en route to head towards the next known Rojas-Gomez-owned business.

***

The remainder of the night, Victor's spots were continuously hit up. His runners and crews were murdered in mass numbers in cold blood; drugs, weapons, and cash were taken and or burned. Victor was beside himself. He felt like he had been sucked into a black hole and couldn't find his way out of it. He couldn't even stand at a toilet and take a piss from how shaky he was.

Sitting in his massive master bedroom of his Naperville condominium, Victor brooded heavily, stuck in his thoughts. It was almost nine in the morning, and frantic calls and texts were still pouring in as his empire was crumbling before his very eyes.

The land-line phone on his nightstand started ringing. Only one person had the number. He dreaded answering it, but he knew if he didn't, the man would show up at his doorstep in a matter of hours.

"¿Si, papa?" he answered, wearily.

"Victor! What the hell is going on up there, mijo?!" yelled Alejandro Rojas-Gomez, creator of the cartel his son now reigned over.

"I know not of what you speak, sir," Victor replied sarcastically, groaning and rubbing his forehead at the same time.

"¡Pendejo! Why am I hearing that you are losing everything because you keep fucking with that Valdez kid?"

"He started it," Victor said.

"¡Pinche idiota! You are fucking up all that I worked hard to establish! What would your abuelita think?!"

"Grandma is in a damn mansion gettin' her old crusty-ass feet rubbed by a guy that wasn't even born when she had *you*! Why do I care what *she* thinks?"

"Without her, mijo, there would be no me, and that means, there would be no you, stupid! Now I have to try to reach out to Juanito and Diego Valdez to *try* and smooth things over, before they end up burying my only fucking son! If I hear *one* more thing about you fucking with that kid, or his family, I promise you, you are cut off! ¡¿Comprendes, cabrón?!"

Victor grinded his teeth in anger. "Yeah, pop. I understand."

The line went dead then. Victor hung the phone back up and immediately grabbed his iPhone. He placed a call to the man that was supposed to have taken the young Dominican out.

Victor waited for an answer. One did not come. He called again, and again, then again. Voicemail only. He decided to send the head sicario a text message.

For a man that calls himself Diablo, there seems to be no evil in you at all. How does a fucking little kid escape this so-called wrath you claim to have. If I do not hear back from you soon, pendejo, you will regret it.

He sent the message then leaned back in his chair, back to brooding. Javier Valdez was still alive. He *had* to do something about it, because *now*, Victor knew if he *didn't*, the Dominicans would get him first. And he knew for a fact that not one of the Valdez killed simply by just bullets. They liked to inflict as much pain as possible on their enemies, *and* their enemies' loved ones.

Victor cringed at the thought of some of the stories that he had heard about those that had been stricken down by the Valdez family. They were certified nuts.

CHAPTER 19
XXXX

Penelope finished her morning coffee and was ready to get to work. She had a lot on her agenda today. She had been paid handsomely to do a job, and she realized that she had only done it half-assed. The woman that had put $100,000 in her hands, just for her to keep information on her boss flowing, was livid. Penelope was now on a mission to prove her worth. She knew if she didn't, she was dead.

The beautiful 5'0" Guatemalan woman was dressed professionally in office attire as normal, though her real profession wasn't even close to office work. She was a street chick that knew people, and those connections got her gigs that paid her a bag.

Penelope was dressed in a dark red suede form-fitting Dolce & Gabbana dress that had black roses embroidered all over it, with a low cleavage line that gave off a teasing view of the tops of her perky little breasts, and an above-the-knee hem line with a slit that went up her left thigh to her hip. Her legs were freshly waxed and oiled up. On her feet she wore pumps that matched her dress. Her hair was flat-ironed and pulled back into a tight bun. Black Gucci glasses framed her slim face. Gold earrings dangled from her ears, matching the necklace around her neck, and the ladies Rolex on her wrist. She wore dark-red eye shadow on her lids, and dark-red lipstick, and had finished herself off a little Chanel No. 5

perfume. She had plans to get herself even closer to her boss, and that meant putting herself out there to him even more than she already had.

After she refilled her coffee thermos, Penelope grabbed her handbag and the keys to her new sporty red Ferrari 458 Italia which sat right outside of her palatial miniature mansion's side door, waiting for her to hop in and go.

She headed to the door, unlocked it and opened it. The second she saw the gigantic tiger-striped dog standing there, she screamed at the tops of her lungs.

The dog immediately pounced on her and took her to the floor with ease, being that he was double her size.

"Oh my God!" Penelope screamed as he growled viciously, drool dropping from his mouth, splattering on her face. "Heelp! Somebody heeellp! Pleeeaassee!"

He sharp teeth were just inches from her face. Penelope was so scared that her bowels evacuated.

"Pablo! ¡Ya!"

Penelope then heard the voice of the one woman who could be someone's best friend, or their worst enemy. Being that she was currently laid out on her back, under a huge killer dog that could likely eat her, Penelope assumed that for her, it was now the latter.

***

CHACHA

Stepping into Penelope's kitchen, ChaCha closed and locked the door behind her. She gave her Dogo Canario the command to fall back. Pablo obeyed and got off the tiny woman. Not a moment after he was back at her side, did ChaCha get a whiff of the foul odor coming from the petrified mole that she had planted in Victor Gomez's trucking firm.

As Penelope went to sit up, ChaCha heard wet squishy sounds. She looked up at ChaCha, with fear in her eyes. Her bladder then released, and pool of dark brown and yellow liquid formed under her.

"Ch-Ch-ChaCha... wh-what's g-g-going on?" Penelope stammered like she was freezing her ass off.

"I paid you to report *everything* to me that hijo de la gran puta was planning to me!" ChaCha growled between clenched teeth. "My two little cousins almost died last night when Victor sent a hit crew at him and his novia, and they were completely in the dark about it because *you* failed to do the job, I paid you one hundred thousand fucking dollars to do!"

Penelope's eyes went wide in shock. "W-Wait! I didn't know! I swear! He never mentioned anything like that in the office, nor anywhere else in the building! I have the whole place bugged, ChaCha!"

ChaCha stepped past Penelope, not wanting to hear another word. Penelope flinched when she got close to her. Pablo snapped at Penelope and made her shriek.

Going to the stove, ChaCha turned on one of the burners.

"ChaCha! Please! Don't hurt me! Please! I can do better! I swear to God I can!" Penelope begged.

ChaCha marched back towards her. Penelope attempted to try and crawl away, but ChaCha caught her by her hair and yanked her up from the floor and started dragging her towards the stove.

"No, no, no, nooo! ChaChaaa! Nooo! Pleassssee!"

Ignoring her cries for mercy, ChaCha muscled the girl to the stove and mashed her face down into the fire. Penelope's blood-curdling scream had no effect on ChaCha. Pablo stood by and watched his human burn the girl's face up.

Penelope tried like hell to fight her way out of ChaCha's hold, but the colomborriqueña was was stronger and bigger than Penelope could have imagined.

ChaCha held Penelope's face in the fire, using all her strength to keep her right there. Almost twenty seconds later, the fight left Penelope, as her soul left her body.

She let go of the dead woman then. Penelope's corpse hit the floor. ChaCha turned on the oven to 500-degrees, then she opened the door, pulled out all the racks inside, grabbed the body and stuffed it inside, closing the door. She then looked at her dog and smiled at him.

"¡Buen trabajo, papa!" she cooed to him. "¿Tienes hambre?" she then asked.

Trained in English and in Spanish, Pablo barked when he she asked if he was hungry.

ChaCha went to Penelope's refrigerator and found almost a whole ham inside. She grabbed it out and held it up for her big hungry dog. Pablo's tail wagged fast; ears perked straight up. Smiling at him, ChaCha set the ham on the floor, then she stepped back about a foot. She then told him to eat and watched him rush the ham and tear into it like it would sprout legs and take off running from him.

While he ripped and pulled chunks of it away, chomping it up like it was his last meal, ChaCha turned and looked at the oven. She went to it and turned the light on inside of it. Penelope's body was already cooking like a Thanksgiving turkey, but it in no way shape or form smelled as delicious as one.

"Goddamn that bitch stinks, yo. Pablo, come on before I throw up," ChaCha said, wrinkling her nose at the putrid smell of piss, shit, and flesh baking.

Pablo bit down on the remainder of the ham he had left and carried it with him, following ChaCha out of the house, leaving the dead girl in the stove to be discovered by fire fighters when her body turned into a blazing ball of flames that would burn the mini mansion down.

CHAPTER 20
KENZIE

Kenzie woke up a few hours after the crazy ordeal, to discover that she and her daughter were wrapped up in the comfy bear fur cover in the big sleeper of Xavier's W900L. The huge 86" studio sleeper, mounted to the truck behind the cab was so big and luxurious that Kenzie had forgotten that she and Neveah were in a semi-truck.

The electrical power was on, enabling the music to be on, and the a/c to keep them cool from the hot summer heat that was backing Illinois. She didn't know that Javi had turned on the truck's small diesel-powered *APU* generator that was mounted to the driver's side of the truck, right on the frame, which provided them power for all the amenities the house on ten wheels had.

She laid there for a minute, in deep thought. She replayed the events of earlier in her head. Her mind raced like a drag racer. The early days of the times when she was with her daughter's father, she had always had a thing for the bad boys, as most women did, secretly or not. Seeing Xavier jump out of his truck like a G with such a big gun, on straight beast mode, to go help his brother out, had Kenzie thinking some very hot things about him.

It was more than that, though, to her. Kenzie admired how down for his family that Xavier was. He was a true rider, and he had a big heart, obviously. The day that he had come into her and Neveah's life, after Kenzie's baby daddy had beat her so badly and threw her through the glass patio door to her apartment out in Zion, had been the day that she felt safe, more than she had in a *very* long time. She was so comfortable around him and could barely hold back her smile when she looked at him. Her daughter even adored him. The way she ran to Xavier, Kenzie hadn't even seen her do *that* with her biological father.

Kenzie was seriously digging on Xavier, and it scared the hell out of her, because she had no clue how he would react *when* he found out about her... *problem*, which he would at some point.

Neveah was still sleeping peacefully, much to Kenzie's surprise. She thought for sure that her little girl would be barely able to sleep, and when she did, she was sure that Neveah would wake up screaming from night terrors.

Kenzie smiled at her little multi-heritage angel. Out of all the things that had come out of her relationship with Stacks, Neveah was *the* best thing.

Just then, a few soft knocks on the driver's door of the truck got Kenzie's attention, then she heard it open. She pulled her eyes away from her daughter and looked forward to where the cab was. She heard his voice a second later.

"Hey, Kenzie? You up? It's me."

A giant smile formed on her face when she heard his voice. It filled her with joy. Her nipples got hard out of nowhere. Butterflies fluttered around in her stomach, tickling her insides.

She could feel the truck shake a little then. A second later, she saw his incredibly handsome cocoa-brown face, before the rest of him stepped up inside of the truck.

Instantly, Kenzie grew aroused. Just the sight of him was enough to get her engine running and humming. He was as much a man as he wanted to be, and it had her swooning.

Even though he was a man of few words, he was the type that didn't need to say much, like so many other dudes out there that boasted about who they claimed they were, knowing they were capping their asses off. Everything about Xavier, it spoke for him, and his swag was so official and alluring, yet so simple, and humble. To her, Xavier was the type of man that commanded respect, and got all eyes on him, without even trying.

Unable to control her excitement, Kenzie climbed up out of the bed, maneuvering over her daughter, then she hopped up and ran to him. Kenzie flung herself into his arms, and before she even realized what she was doing, she had pulled him down and her lips were pressed against his.

She was as surprised by her kissing him as he *felt* like he was. She had an aggressive sexual nature that barely ever came out, but Xavier seemed to bring everything in her out, without even knowing it. He made her feel things that she couldn't remember another man ever making her feel.

Kenzie wanted him in the worst way ever. She had to admit it to herself. The red-hot desire that she had for him burned so deeply inside of her that she could melt and crave for him to lick her up.

***

XAVIER

He was truly taken aback by Kenzie's explosive display of affection. It was very welcome, but he had *not* expected it at all.

As Kenzie kissed him, he couldn't help it that his hands wanted to feel that big fat juicy 48" donk that he had secretly being dying to know the feeling of. His hands slid down her sides and cupped it, squeezing it. The red leggings that she had on made it look so much fatter than it was, and it felt so soft. Xavier felt his dick hardening in his 501s at the thought of what it would look like without the leggings, clapping in his face.

188

He met her hungerful kiss with his own and thrust his tongue into her mouth. He explored her, squeezing her ass and caressing her meaty booty cheeks.

Kenzie moaned from the kiss, and from how good his lips felt, and how good his hands felt cupping and rubbing her ass. She could feel her panties getting wet, and her temperature rose. Her kitty was purring, craving for him to stroke her.

After nearly a minute long kiss, she pulled back, feeling bashfully shy now. She was embarrassed that she had just attacked him, without even thinking. But when she looked up into his soft soulful brown eyes, and saw his million-dollar smile peeking, she wanted to kiss him again and never stop.

"Well… that was a very nice '*Hey, papi, whaz' hanin'*," he joked, with a chuckle that made Kenzie cheese up.

She started blushing so hard. He could tell that she was embarrassed, but still, she had that look in her eyes that said she would not hesitate to go beyond lip boxing.

"Oh… um… heeeey, papi, whaz' happeniiiin'," Kenzie then said, curling her hands together, barely able to look at him, out of fear of absent-mindedly jumping onto *his* shifter, and putting *him* into gear.

Xavier busted out laughing at her cheeks getting red. "Yo' ass cray-cray, lil' mama," he told her, taking her hand and pulling her to him. "pero, esa 'mielda me gusta, mamita," he added.

Kenzie got goose bumps from how low his voice just got and though she had never learned Spanish from the Cuban side of her family, hearing him speak it had her yearning for him to say more. It drove her crazy.

"I'm s-sorry… I don't know what just came over me," she capped, feeling the wetness between her legs.

"*I* do," Xavier told her, reaching down and tipping her chin up with a finger, so he could look down into her glistening eyes. "You got chu' a *real* nigga in yo' life now.

You know real when you see real, so you movin' in to stake yo' claim. I say bravo to that, ma. Women that go after what they want are sexy as *fuck* to me."

"*Ahem*! Aye, nigga!"

Maaaaan, come on, yo! Xavier thought, when he heard her voice behind him.

Feeling like his stomach had just dropped due to knowing that she was right behind him, Xavier turned, and saw the wild-ass Nena, standing right outside of his truck, arms folded across her bosom, looking so pissed off that she might start breathing fire.

***

MICHELLE

Michelle moaned out at the tops of her lungs, back arching up off the bed, her toes curling, eyes squeezed shut, then she exploded, all in Javi's face, drenching it with her sweet nectar. Javi licked her clean after he ate the pussy up so good that Michelle felt like he was *still* sucking on her clit.

They were both naked, hidden away in the tall spacious aerodyne-style sleeper berth in one of his spare trucks, a Kenworth T660 with a luxurious interior and a deluxe sleeper.

Javi had no hesitation at all when his woman said she didn't want to go home, nor to a hotel, but to his KW to rest and wait for the word to come from ChaCha and the rest of the mob that was putting their murder game down on Victor Gomez's associates.

Demon and Diamond were outside of the truck, protecting their territory and enjoying the beautiful summer weather while they ran around on patrol-mode.

"¡Maldita sea, Javier!" Michelle exclaimed, trying to catch her breath. "You and those fucking lips, man! ¡Coño, papi!"

Javi withdrew his face from between her thick thighs and climbing up on top of her, he gave her a wet-lipped smile that made her bust out laughing at him.

"You know *damn* well you *love* it when I go in on yo' ass wit' these-," he started to say.

He and Michelle both heard the dogs barking, but more than them, they could hear someone yelling, screaming, and cursing.

"What the hell? That sounds like... oh shit," Javi said, cursing as he realized who was going ballistic.

"Nena," Michelle finished for him.

Then they heard Xavier shouting for her to stop. Right after, they heard Kenzie shouting.

"Dammit! What the fuck is goin' out on there?!" asked Javi, already hurrying to get his clothes and boots back on.

They both quickly got dressed and jumped out of the truck. They saw Demon and Diamond first, with Precious next to them, barking in the direction of where the W900L that Kenzie and Neveah had fallen asleep in was.

Right outside of Xavier's truck, they saw Kenzie and Nena, squaring off with each other. Xavier was between them, trying to keep his honey-dip and his new chick from tearing each other up.

"I got a honcho on Kenzie," Michelle told Javi on the low, as they made their way over to the dramatic scene.

"No deal. Kenzie will tear Ms. Pilsen's little ass up," Javi said, trying to hide the smile of anticipation that threatened to come out.

***

KENZIE

"Come on, *bitch*! All that woofin' yo' ass just did?! Run up and get *rocked*, hoe!" Kenzie snapped, trying to get around Xavier.

"Kenzie! Chill ma!" he shouted, looking back and forth from Nena to Kenzie, not for a second missing the significant difference in height between the two.

Nena seized the opportunity, the next time that he looked away from her. She ducked under his arm and popped up on Kenzie; Kenzie saw her and jumped back, gunned up. She swung a hard right hook, but having underestimated the yellow-bone's ability to box, Kenzie missed, then her head snapped upwards when Nena's left came and hit her with an upper-cut that was so hard it sent Kenzie backwards to the ground.

Xavier was shocked as he managed to grab Nena and push her away from Kenzie, who had gotten right back up as fast as she went down.

"Nena! Stop, yo! Both of y'all!" Xavier roared, trying hard to keep them back, now as angry as a bull being taunted with a red flag.

Kenzie pulled it then. She got around Xavier, giving him the slip. He tried to catch her, but she ducked him and went clean in on Nena, throwing four lightning-fast punches that flipped the script and had *Nena*, now on her ass.

Suddenly, Michelle appeared, right in front of Kenzie as she was about to jump on Nena and flood her. Xavier hurried and grabbed Kenzie, pulling her away, while Javi managed to catch Nena as she jumped up to keep at it.

"Let me go! Let me gooo!" Nena screamed, trying her hardest to get free of Javi's grasp.

Kenzie was still trying to get free of Xavier, even as he carried her away. As they got closer to his truck, she heard Neveah crying, which immediately took her mind off beating Nena up and being a mother.

She gasped, leaving beast mode. Her daughter's cries got her to break free of Xavier, mostly when he let her go, when he saw she was trying to get to her little girl, and not Nena. When he set her down, Kenzie took off to the truck and jumped up inside, swooping her daughter up into her arms and cradling her.

Xavier watched her rock her little one back and forth for a minute, doing her best to comfort Neveah, then he turned around to see his brother and Michelle, trying to get Nena to cool out. Javi looked his way a second later, then he shook his head.

***

MICHELLE

"Nena, I swear to God, if you don't chill out, yo," Michelle said, while Javi had her wrapped up, and their dogs stood by, watching. "What the hell is wrong with you?"

"Heer!" Nena's eyes went in the direction of where Kenzie now had her daughter outside of the truck, with Xavier and Precious at her side. "That white bitch stole my man from me!"

"*Azalia!*" Michelle snapped, calling Nena by her government name. "He was *not* ya' fuckin' man, girl! Yo, y'all was fuckin', pendeja! That was it! Get it through 'ya head and move *oooon*! ¡*Coño*!"

Michelle saw Nena look over at where Xavier stood with his dog, the red head, and the little girl.

"So that's all I was to you, Xavier?! Just some *pussy*?!" she shouted at him.

"Nena! Watch yo' mouth! There's a freakin' kid hearin' you!" Javi scolded her.

Xavier cautiously approached, leaving Kenzie and her daughter for a minute. Precious trotted alongside with him.

"You know better than that, Nena," he told her, talking to her with a softer tone of voice. "You been my friend for a long time, and somewhere down the line, we started gettin' intimate. We both said before we did the dirty, that there were not gon' be no strings attached, and that we wasn't gon' catch feelings. What happened to that?"

"Man, *fuck* all that other shit, nigga! I caught feelings!" she admitted, keeping it a buck. "But you already knew that, Xavier!"

Nena then burst into tears Javi let her go and she fell to her knees, crying her eyes out.

Michelle was beyond puzzled by all the crazy emotions spewing out of Nena. She was crazy, but this was a whole new level for her. Nobody had ever seen her break down the way she was now.

She looked over at where Kenzie was. She saw that she had managed to get her daughter to stop crying. She held Neveah to her chest, while leaning against Xavier's truck, looking their way.

"Nena?"

Michelle looked back and saw Xavier was gently pulling her back up from the ground.

"Talk to me, ma. Why is you buggin' so hard right now.

Michelle was wondering the same thing, as she was sure Javi was too.

Nena looked at Xavier with red teary eyes. "Because… I'm pregnant and it's your baby! That's why dickhead!" she snapped, then she yanked all the way free of Xavier, ran to the 1996 Chevy Caprice bubble-body on chromed Forgiato deuces that Xavier had given her, after her new Benz broke down, jumped inside and started the beefed-up 350 cubic-inch V8 under the hood.

Nena slammed it in drive and mashed the gas. She peeled off and flew up out of the yard. Her engine roared out of the Flowmaster exhaust pipes, sounding as angry as the pregnant woman behind the wheel.

Michelle looked at Xavier. She saw his jaw was damn near on the ground and his eyes looked like they might pop out of their sockets.

Over where Kenzie was, Michelle saw the red head had the same expression on her face, and Javi wore the same look of shock on his mug as well.

"Wow," she heard Xavier say, after nearly a whole minute of silence had passed between them all. "Um… anybody care to tell me that she didn't just tell me that?"

"Not sure that's possible, Xavier," said Michelle, "but what I *can* say to you is… *oooowwweee*! You shoulda' strapped up, my nigga, 'cause now… you really *are* hers."

Xavier took a deep breath, and then he exhaled, then, under his breath, he cursed, kicking his own ass mentally for slipping up so badly.

CHAPTER 21
JAVI

"That's wild, yo… Nena is gonna' have your first niece, or nephew," said Michelle, still in a state of shock by the news.

She and Javi were up in a private room up inside of the garage, of which most people didn't even know existed.

The news was not anything that anyone could have anticipated. Nobody disliked or hated Nena in any way. She was loved dearly, but she was crazy, and was known to fly off the deep end, real quick.

Javi shook his head at it. "Well… at least the baby won't be a punk-ass little kid when he, or she gets a little older. That upper cut was not expected."

Michelle chuckled. "No, it most definitely wasn't, but Kenzie got her little ass, just like we thought."

"Well, Kenzie's damn near my height, and Nena is, like, an inch taller than you; reach plays a real big role in boxin' heads up."

"Uh huh. I'm hungry. Let's shower and get fresh then go get some food," Michelle suggested.

"Sounds like a good idea. You drained all my energy in the truck," Javi said with a laugh, right as his phone rang.

He looked at the screen and saw it was an old family friend calling.

"Eeeee, El Sol is calling," Javi said, then answered the call. "Dimelo, venezolano," he said.

"What's up, young man. Any chance you got someone that can come help me get rid of a little bit of this waste? My tanks are full," said Sol.

"I certainly can, my good man. How soon?"

"As soon as possible. This is… an expensive ask, so you'll be happy with the commas that come with it."

"Say less, Viejo. I'll be on the way in a few hours."

"Cool. See you then, Javi," said Sol, then he ended the call.

"Sol needs his tanks emptied, and I am not exactly excited to know what muck it is inside of it," Javi said, remembering the last time he had hauled out the residual waste that Sol stockpiled until it was time to take it away.

Michelle shivered from the thought, as she had gone with him. "Nasty, I'd definitely say," she replied, "but he pays very handsomely, so fuck it. The money is the motive, right, papi?"

"Siempre, amor. Now let's go get cleaned up and head out," Javi told her.

After they hopped into their private shower, Javi got dressed in a pair of Balenciaga jeans with cuts in them, with a Balenciaga shirt, and fresh all-white Air Jordan 1s on his feet.

Michelle slipped her shapely bottom half into a pair of super tight and shiny Givenchy leather pants, with a white Givenchy shirt, and a pair of pointed-toe stilettos that were black and shiny like her pants. She put her hair up into a high ponytail, gave herself smokey eyes and applied red lipstick. After she put on her big white-gold hoop earrings and a white-gold necklace, she was ready to go.

"Goooooooo*daaamn*, that ass is *fat*! Wooo!" shouted Javi, as she walked in front of him towards the stairs that led back down to the main service area.

Michelle laughed as he played patti-cake with her booty cheeks. "Javi, leave my butt alone before I make you put your face in it, yo."

"That is a threat I would loooove you to make good on! Like right now!"

"Boy, would you just come on! Damn! Fuckin' booty freak!"

With Demon and Diamond, Javi and Michelle headed towards his 2009 Cadillac Escalade Ext pick-up. It sported a Root Beer candy-paint job with exclusive peanut-butter colored leather interior. It sat high up on 30" Forgiatos that cost as much as the six-year-old SUV.

Javi's phone started ringing. As he pulled it out of his pocket to answer it, he saw Xavier helping Kenzie getting Neveah into her car seat that he had in the rear row of his blacked-out 2013 Range Rover HSE Supercharged, while Precious sat obediently next to his leg.

"Dimelo, primo," Javi said, answering his big cousin's call.

"Yo, lil' cutty, y'all good?" came Danny's voice.

"Yeah, we cool, cuz. Mrs. Green got Michelle back together. We about to head out to get some breakfast real quick, and at some point, I'm expectin' a visit from Johnny Law to slide past about my stolen truck, ya dig I'm sayin'?"

"I hear you. Make sure you keep ya' lady close to you, lil cutty. Homiez, cuz. You two got real lucky; no more underestimatin' when and where shit can go down. ¿Me entiendes? Ain't shit cool out there 'til dude's bitchass is pushin' flowers in a dump somewhere."

"I know. Believe me, cuz, ChaCha been tellin' me the same thing, repeatedly."

Danny chuckled. "You's a hardhead, so I told her stay on your ass; both of y'all's asses. Aye, you gon' need to take somethin' to Perry soon. I'll let you know when."

"Word?" Javi asked.

As Danny went to reply, Javi saw a charcoal-gray Dodge Charger with darkly tinted windows turn into his yard. He and Michelle's eye went to the license plate in front of the car and saw it was white with green numbers and letters.

"Yo', cuzzo, five-o just rolled into my yard. Lemme' get at you a lil' later, aight?" Javi said, as the unmarked Lake County Sheriff's vehicle rolled up to where he and his woman and their dogs were standing.

"Yeah. Make sure you get the pig's name; if he gives you any extra shit, you already know what to do, right?"

"Claro que si, cuzzo."

"Cool. Cuidate, primo, and give Michelle my love, yo," Danny said then.

"Fa' sho, cuz, I will, and you be careful, too. Love, cuz."

"One," Danny said to that, then the call ended.

Michelle stood by her man's side. Their dogs positioned themselves in front of them, looking at the Charger as it came to a stop about ten feet away from them.

Javi glanced over at where his brother and the ladies were. He saw that they were looking at the cop car as well, while Precious sat in the Range Rover, keeping Neveah company.

The Charger's driver door opened seconds later. Out came a hefty, brown-skinned Hispanic man, wearing a suit. The top of his head was bare of any hair, but on his face, he wore a thick *Pancho Villa*-style mustache. He stood a few inches shorter than Javi, but was wide at the shoulders, and out at the stomach. He looked to be in his 50's or so, due to the salt-n-pepper hair that he had around the sides and back of his head.

Demon and Diamond started growling as the man turned around and looked all around the Dedicated Transport yard, Xavier and Kenzie, then turning back and looking at Javi and Michelle.

Michelle told the dogs to relax. They went quiet, but still, they kept their eyes on the stranger that had come into their territory.

Javi knew that their dogs sensed good and bad in people. They didn't get aggressive just because someone was a stranger.

Javi peeped his brother making his way over just then, to come and stand with his big bro and Michelle, while Kenzie stayed with her daughter and Precious.

The cop looked at Javi, Xavier, and Michelle then. With a smirk, he looked at the dogs. They both started growling again when he looked them in their eyes.

"Could you put a leash on those dogs, sir?" the man asked, hand going towards his holstered gun.

"Yes, I *could*, but I am *not* goin' to," Javi told him straight up. "This is *my* property, which makes it *theirs*, too. You weren't invited here; I was told you would meet us somewhere else."

The man shrugged his shoulders. "I was in the neighborhood and thought I'd stop by. Any who, I'm Detective Martin Barrera, with the Lake County Sheriff's department. I assume that you are Señor Javier Valdez?"

"He is *I* and I am *him*," Javi replied sarcastically.

Xavier caught a very bad vibe from the cop. Michelle did, too. It was like the man was possessed by evil spirits.

"Well, sir, it's very nice to finally meet whom I have heard so much about; you and your, uh… family."

Javi smirked at him. "All good things, I hope?"

"Ha! Yeah, anyways. So, your, uh, Kenworth big rig has been recovered. It had been rolled over up in Racine, close to Caledonia, Wisconsin, on Interstate 94. It's been involved in some serious crimes. Lots of dead bodies belonging to a Mexican sicario's hit crew. Previously, we discovered that it had also been involved in a high-speed chase with two other big rigs," Detective Barrera told him, watching Javi's facial expression, which to his surprise, stayed neutral for the most part. "One driver," he continued, "was shot in the face by what *had* to be an automatic weapon; the other," he again paused, peeping the smirk on Michelle's face, "had been determined to have hit his face so hard on the steering wheel, when he crashed into something really hard, that pieces of his skull broke and punctured the front of his brain. He was dead on impact."

"¡Coño!" Javi chuckled. "Yo, that sounds like some shit you'd see in a movie! Someone did *all* that in *my* truck?!"

The detective chuckled. "It appears that way, sir. I don't suppose it was you driving, huh?"

"Nope. Someone that can drive *real* good did *that* shit."

Xavier and Michelle snickered.

"Hmmm." The detective nodded his head, chuckling himself. "Funny thing is, Mr. Valdez, is that only your fingerprints were on the steering wheel and the shifter."

"Gloves," Javi told him. "Car... I mean... truck thieves, best friends, feel me?"

"Oh, I feel you." Detective Barrera looked at Michelle. "Looks like you have a little owie. No chance that your blood would match what we found in the cab, right, ma'am?"

"Nope." Michelle smiled him."Aye, yo, my man." Tired of the cop's presence, Xavier stepped in. "I think my brother and his woman would like to go home and get some rest, so how 'bout you do yo' dumbass report so we can file an insurance claim, then you hop 'ya ass back in that cheap-ass Charger and scoot!"

Detective Barrera smirked at Xavier. "Sure. No problem, young man."

The detective did his report but took his time placing the pen back into his breast pocket. He then smiled at the three, then at Javi.

"I'd be very careful if I were you, Mr. Valdez. You have a very dangerous enemy after you. Take care now, sir," he said.

"Dangerous enemy these nuts, pig," Javi told him, smirking back at the cop as he headed back to his car. "¡Metetelo por *culo*, mamahuevo!" he added.

They all watched him hop back into his Charger and leave out of the yard. Through the chain-link fence lining the front of the yard, they watched the car ride down Frontage Road, and hit a left onto Russell, then disappear from their line of sight.

"He knows something," Michelle surmised, turning and looking at the two. "A cop that knows something is a very dangerous person, y'all."

"And so is some fearless gangsta-ass Afro-Latino niggas wit' guns," Javi replied. "¡Dale banda! Dude can eat a dick!"

Xavier chuckled.

Michelle shook her head.

"Yo, we have all dealt with shit like this before! Fuck is y'all lookin' like that old-ass paisa rattled y'all for?"

Michelle stepped right up to him and looked up into his face. Xavier started snickering to himself, knowing Javi's woman was about to get in his ass.

"Ain't nobody in this whole motherfuckin' world ever can have *me* rattled, Javier! Asi que, hush that shit up, 'cause I'll get on some G-shit wit' cha' ass right here and now, in front of ya' brother and the lil' mamas. Care to try me?"

"No."

Xavier busted out laughing at his brother's face.

"¡Callate!" Javi hissed at him.

"Naw, nigga! Don't get tough wit' *me* 'cause *yo'* ass just got treated! Bang, bang, nigga!" Xavier teased, then he walked off to hop up in his Range and get home, for some much needed rest and recuperation.

Javi looked and saw that his woman was still glaring up at him, with her eyes narrowed. She was daring him to talk crazy. He started smiling at her, taunting her.

"Youn' want no 'shmoke', chiquitita," he told her, putting his forehead to hers,

"Tu quieres que te entre a galleta, Javier," Michelle said, with a smirk growing on her face.

"You talk a lot of shit," he replied, twisting his lips up.

"And I back *all* that shit up, nigga."

"Prove it, punk."

"After I get some food in my stomach, I will, *punk*," she playfully shot back, then she head-butted him.

"And they say that I'm the one that's hardheaded," Javi said, then he scooped his woman up off of her feet suddenly.

Michelle, taken by surprise, shrieked when she was up in his arms. She giggled like a little love-struck girl as he hurried to get her up into his Caddy truck.

Demon and Diamond jumped up into the rear when he opened the door, then hopping up behind the wheel he started the powerful supercharged engine and dipped off, hungry as hell, and ready to ge this woman to their crib so he could beat it up.

***

XXXX

"On my *crown*, if y'all nigga fuck this up, I'ma snatch y'alls wives and y'alls kids and send they ass to Mexico and sell 'em to the creepiest paisa for a fuckin' peso! DO NOT MISS!"

Rodrigo and Carmelo did not like the threat issued by their big homie, but they knew for a fact, that he was not joking.

"Aight, King. We won't miss.," Carmelo said as Rodrigo followed the root-beer colored Escalade from a distance, with his Mac 11 on his lap, and Carmelo with twin Uzis. "ain't no *way* they gettin' away from us. We two cars behind them and they don't even know we comin', joe."

"You heard what I said, nigga. Get the shit done and you gon' get paid that half-million that ol' boy put on that nigga Javi's head, then y'all two can go on a long vacation."

The call ended with nothing more said.

"Man, fuck this waitin' shit, nigga! Let's do this shit, King! Right *now*!" said Rodrigo, as he followed the Cadillac truck on the curved entrance way to Illinois Route 41.

Once on the highway, he and Carmelo kept their eyes on the SUV. They both glanced at the truck weight station that they were about to pass on their right, meant for south bound commercial traffic. They saw it was closed, which meant no Illinois State Police manning it. Glad that no cops would interfere, Rodrigo put his eyes back on the Escalade, seeing it come to a stop at a red light at 41 and Route 173.

"Get ready, King. I finna pull up; you pop they ass and we out! Simple! Got it?" he said to Carmelo.

"On 360, I got it, brotha'. Let's go!"

***

JAVI

"Woooooo… ooooohhhh fuuuuuck! Goddamn, baby!" Javi groaned, as Michelle sucked and jerked his cock like a porn star.

On her knees in her seat, she deep throated him, with her ass up in the air. Javi rubbed and caressed her fat round rear end through the shiny leather fabric of her pants, smacking on it. His eyes rolled to the back of his head, and she went harder on him. She moaned and took all of him to the back of her throat with ease. Javi could feel his nuts tightening up as his nut started building up. His toes curled in his Mikes.

He squeezed his eyes shut as his nut started rising. He groaned, ready to bust. Michelle could feel his cock spasming in her throat. She started jerking him with one hand, making Javi curse and groan even louder.

"¡Cono! I f-f-finna b-buss'!" he announced.

TAP TAP TAP

Right before his nut came, Javi heard three loud taps on his window. He and Michelle nearly jumped out of their skins. Demon and Diamond immediately started barking.

Javi looked to his left and found himself looking into the barrels of two Uzis, pointing right at his face, held by a man with a hoodie up and a ski-mask on.

"Javi!" Michelle screamed, seeing the man with the spitters start grinning.

"Game over bitch ass nigga!" he shouted, then he squeezed both triggers.

BRRRRRRRRRRRRRRRRRRRRRRRRRRRRRRRRRRR!

To Be Continued...

Lock Down Publications and Ca$h Presents
Assisted Publishing Packages

Due to an increase in the price of services we have increased our prices. The prices below reflect the price increase as of 11/1/24.

BASIC PACKAGE	UPGRADED PACKAGE
$699	**$1000**
Editing	Typing
Cover Design	Editing
Formatting	Cover Design
	Formatting
	Upload eBooks to Amazon
	Upload Paperback to Amazon
ADVANCE PACKAGE	**LDP SUPREME PACKAGE**
$1,400	**$1,700**
Typing	Typing
Editing (line editing/content)	Editing (line editing/content)
Cover Design	Cover Design
Formatting	Formatting
Copyright Registration	Copyright Registration
Proofreading	Proofreading
Upload eBooks to Amazon	Set up Amazon Account
Upload Paperback to Amazon	Upload eBooks to Amazon
	Upload Paperback to Amazon
	Advertise on LDP's Amazon and Facebook Page

***Other services available upon request.
Additional charges may apply

Lock Down Publications
P.O. Box 944
Stockbridge, GA 30281-9998
Phone: 470 303-9761
Email: lockdownpublications@gmail.com

Submission Guideline

Submit the first three chapters of your completed manuscript to ldpsubmissions@gmail.com. In the subject line add **Your Book's Title**. The manuscript must be in a Word Doc file and sent as an attachment. Document should be in Times New Roman, double spaced, and in size 12 font. Also, provide your synopsis and full contact information. If sending multiple submissions, they must each be in a separate email.

Have a story but no way to send it electronically? You can still submit to LDP/Ca$h Presents. Send in the first three chapters, written or typed, of your completed manuscript to:

LDP: Submissions Dept
P.O. Box 944
Stockbridge, GA 30281-9998

DO NOT send original manuscript. Must be a duplicate.
Provide your synopsis and a cover letter containing your full contact information.

Thanks for considering LDP and Ca$h Presents.

NEW RELEASES

BLOODLINE OF A SAVAGE 1,2&3
THESE VICIOUS STREETS 1,2&3
RELENTLESS GOON
RELENTLESS GOON 2
BY PRINCE A. TAUHID

THE BUTTERFLY MAFIA 1-3
BY FUMIYA PAYNE

A THUG'S STREET PRINCESS 1,2&3
BY MEESHA

CITY OF SMOKE 1& 2
BY MOLOTTI

STEPPERS 1,2&3
THE REAL BADDIES OF CHI-RAQ
BY KING RIO

THE LANE 1&2
BY KEN-KEN SPENCE

THUG OF SPADES 1,2&3
LOVE IN THE TRENCHES 2
CORNER BOY CHRONICLES
BY COREY ROBINSON

TIL DEATH 3
BY ARYANNA

THE BIRTH OF A GANGSTER 4
BY DELMONT PLAYER

PRODUCT OF THE STREETS 1&2
BY DEMOND "MONEY" ANDERSON

NO TIME FOR ERROR
BY KEESE

MONEY HUNGRY DEMONS 1,2&3
BY TRANAY ADAMS

HUNGRY FOR MONEY 1&2
BY SLIMBOS

A THUGGISH PASSION
KILLAZ ON STANDBY 1&2
LAND OF DA HOOLIGANZ 1,2&3
FRESH OFF DA PORCH
BY IRA B.

COUNTDOWN OF A KILLA 1&2
GUNS DOWN, BOTTOMS UP 1&2
SEX, MURDA AND GOD
BY LO-LIFE

THE LEVEL UP 1&2
BY LUXURY KING

FO'EVA ROLLIN' 1&2
BY ASSA RAYMOND BAKER

HUB CITY MENACE 1&2
BY J. WHITE

KILLA CREW
DYING FOR LIKES
BY ARYANNA

IF YOU CROSS ME ONCE 6
ANGEL 5
By Anthony Fields

IMMA DIE BOUT MINE 5
By Aryanna

A THUGS STREET PRINCESS 3
EMBRACING THE LOVE OF A BOSS
By Meesha

PRODUCT OF THE STREETS 3
By Demond Money Anderson

STANDING ON HER BUSINESS
BY DG SANTANA

GET IT IN SLUGS 1&2
B. STALLS

CORNER BOYS 2
By Corey Robinson

THE MURDER QUEENS 6&7
By Michael Gallon

CITY OF SMOKE 3
By Molotti

CONFESSIONS OF A DOPEBOY
By Nicholas Lock

TENDER
BY KHUFU

THA TAKEOVER
By Keith Chandler

BETRAYAL OF A G 2
By Ray Vinci

CRIME BOSS 4
By Playa Ray

Coming Soon from Lock Down Publications/Ca$h Presents

RAN OFF ON THE PLUG 2 by **PAPER BOI RARI**
STREET REDEMPTION by **TONY DANIELS**
SAVAGE FAMILY EMPIRE by **PRINCE TAUHID**
BAD BITCHES WIT' GUNZ by **DIESEL**
THE SINGLE LADIES by **DIESEL**
COKE BY THE TRUCKLOAD by **DIESEL**
PROBLEM SOLVED by **DIESEL**
TIPPIN' THE SCALES by **DIESEL**
OPPS CRY TOO by **SAYNOMORE**
A GANGSTA'S KARMA by **FLAME**

AVAILABLE NOW

RESTRAINING ORDER 1 & 2
By **CA$H & Coffee**

LOVE KNOWS NO BOUNDARIES 1-3
By **Coffee**

RAISED AS A GOON I, II, III & IV
BRED BY THE SLUMS I, II, III
BLAST FOR ME I & II
ROTTEN TO THE CORE I II III
A BRONX TALE I, II, III
DUFFLE BAG CARTEL I II III IV V VI
HEARTLESS GOON I II III IV V
A SAVAGE DOPEBOY I II
DRUG LORDS I II III
CUTTHROAT MAFIA I II
KING OF THE TRENCHES
By **Ghost**

LAY IT DOWN I & II
LAST OF A DYING BREED I II
BLOOD STAINS OF A SHOTTA I & II III
By **Jamaica**

LOYAL TO THE GAME I II III
LIFE OF SIN I, II III
By **TJ & Jelissa**

IF LOVING HIM IS WRONG…I & II
LOVE ME EVEN WHEN IT HURTS I II III
By **Jelissa**

PUSH IT TO THE LIMIT
By **Bre' Hayes**

BLOODY COMMAS I & II
SKI MASK CARTEL I, II & III
KING OF NEW YORK I II, III IV V
RISE TO POWER I II III
COKE KINGS I II III IV V
BORN HEARTLESS I II III IV
KING OF THE TRAP I II
By **T.J. Edwards**

WHEN THE STREETS CLAP BACK I & II III
THE HEART OF A SAVAGE I II III IV
MONEY MAFIA I II
LOYAL TO THE SOIL I II III
By **Jibril Williams**

A DISTINGUISHED THUG STOLE MY HEART I - III
LOVE SHOULDN'T HURT I II III IV
RENEGADE BOYS 1-4
PAID IN KARMA 1-3
SAVAGE STORMS 1-3
AN UNFORESEEN LOVE 1-3
BABY, I'M WINTERTIME COLD 1-3
A THUG'S STREET PRINCESS 1&2
By **Meesha**

CUM FOR ME 1-8
An LDP Erotica Collaboration

BLOOD OF A BOSS 1-5
SHADOWS OF THE GAME
TRAP BASTARD
By **Askari**

A GANGSTER'S CODE 1-3
A GANGSTER'S SYN 1-3
THE SAVAGE LIFE 1-3
CHAINED TO THE STREETS 1-3
BLOOD ON THE MONEY 1-3
A GANGSTA'S PAIN 1-3
BEAUTIFUL LIES AND UGLY TRUTHS
CHURCH IN THESE STREETS
By **J-Blunt**

THE STREETS BLEED MURDER 1-3
THE HEART OF A GANGSTA 1-3
By **Jerry Jackson**

WHEN A GOOD GIRL GOES BAD
By **Adrienne**

THE COST OF LOYALTY 1-3
By **Kweli**

BRIDE OF A HUSTLA 1-3
THE FETTI GIRLS 1-3
CORRUPTED BY A GANGSTA 1-4
BLINDED BY HIS LOVE
THE PRICE YOU PAY FOR LOVE 1-3
DOPE GIRL MAGIC 1-3
By **Destiny Skai**

A KINGPIN'S AMBITION
A KINGPIN'S AMBITION II
I MURDER FOR THE DOUGH
By **Ambitious**

A DOPEBOY'S PRAYER
By **Eddie "Wolf" Lee**

TRUE SAVAGE 1-7
DOPE BOY MAGIC 1-3
MIDNIGHT CARTEL 1-3
CITY OF KINGZ 1&2
NIGHTMARE ON SILENT AVE
THE PLUG OF LIL MEXICO 1&2
CLASSIC CITY
By **Chris Green**

LOVE & CHASIN' PAPER
By **Qay Crockett**

THE KING CARTEL 1-3
By **Frank Gresham**

THESE NIGGAS AIN'T LOYAL 1-3
By **Nikki Tee**

GANGSTA SHYT 1-3
By **CATO**

THE ULTIMATE BETRAYAL
By **Phoenix**

BOSS'N UP 1-3
By **Royal Nicole**

I LOVE YOU TO DEATH
By **Destiny J**

BROOKLYN HUSTLAZ
By **Boogsy Morina**

GANGSTA CITY
By **Teddy Duke**

TO DIE IN VAIN
SINS OF A HUSTLA
By **ASAD**

I RIDE FOR MY HITTA
I STILL RIDE FOR MY HITTA
By **Misty Holt**

A GANGSTER'S REVENGE 1-4
THE BOSS MAN'S DAUGHTERS 1-5
A SAVAGE LOVE 1&2
BAE BELONGS TO ME 1&2
A HUSTLER'S DECEIT 1-3
WHAT BAD BITCHES DO 1-3
SOUL OF A MONSTER 1-3
KILL ZONE
A DOPE BOY'S QUEEN 1-3
TIL DEATH 1-3
IMMA DIE BOUT MINE 1-5
By **Aryanna**

BROOKLYN ON LOCK 1 & 2
By **Sonovia**

A DRUG KING AND HIS DIAMOND 1-3
A DOPEMAN'S RICHES
HER MAN, MINE'S TOO 1&2
CASH MONEY HO'S
THE WIFEY I USED TO BE 1&2
PRETTY GIRLS DO NASTY THINGS
By **Nicole Goosby**

THE STREETS ARE CALLING
By **Duquie Wilson**

LIPSTICK KILLAH 1-3
CRIME OF PASSION 1-3
FRIEND OR FOE 1-3
By **Mimi**

TRAPHOUSE KING 1-3
KINGPIN KILLAZ 1-3
STREET KINGS 1&2
PAID IN BLOOD 1&2
CARTEL KILLAZ 1-3
DOPE GODS 1&2
By **Hood Rich**

STEADY MOBBN' 1-3
THE STREETS STAINED MY SOUL 1-3
By **Marcellus Allen**

WHO SHOT YA 1-3
SON OF A DOPE FIEND 1-4
HEAVEN GOT A GHETTO 1&2
SKI MASK MONEY 1&2
By **Renta**

GORILLAZ IN THE BAY 1-4
TEARS OF A GANGSTA 1/&2
3X KRAZY 1&2
STRAIGHT BEAST MODE 1&2
By **DE'KARI**

TRIGGADALE 1-3
MURDA WAS THE CASE 1-3
By **Elijah R. Freeman**

MARRIED TO A BOSS 1-3
By **Destiny Skai & Chris Green**

SLAUGHTER GANG 1-3
RUTHLESS HEART 1-3
By **Willie Slaughter**

GOD BLESS THE TRAPPERS 1-3
THESE SCANDALOUS STREETS 1-3
FEAR MY GANGSTA 1-5
THESE STREETS DON'T LOVE NOBODY 1-2
BURY ME A G 1-5
A GANGSTA'S EMPIRE 1-4
THE DOPEMAN'S BODYGAURD 1&2
THE REALEST KILLAZ 1-3
THE LAST OF THE OGS 1-3
By **Tranay Adams**

KINGZ OF THE GAME 1-7
CRIME BOSS 1-4
By **Playa Ray**

FUK SHYT
By **Blakk Diamond**

DON'T F#CK WITH MY HEART 1&2
By **Linnea**

ADDICTED TO THE DRAMA 1-3
IN THE ARM OF HIS BOSS
By **Jamila**

LOYALTY AIN'T PROMISED 1&2
By **Keith Williams**

FOREVER GANGSTA 1&2
GLOCKS ON SATIN SHEETS 1&2
By **Adrian Dulan**

YAYO 1-4
A SHOOTER'S AMBITION 1&2
BRED IN THE GAME
By **S. Allen**

TRAP GOD 1-3
RICH $AVAGE 1-3
MONEY IN THE GRAVE 1-3
CARTEL MONEY
By **Martell Troublesome Bolden**

TOE TAGZ 1-4
LEVELS TO THIS SHYT 1&2
IT'S JUST ME AND YOU
By **Ah'Million**

KINGPIN DREAMS 1-3
RAN OFF ON DA PLUG
By **Paper Boi Rari**

THE STREETS MADE ME 1-3
By **Larry D. Wright**

CONFESSIONS OF A GANGSTA 1-4
CONFESSIONS OF A JACKBOY 1-3
CONFESSIONS OF A HITMAN
By **Nicholas Lock**

I'M NOTHING WITHOUT HIS LOVE
SINS OF A THUG
TO THE THUG I LOVED BEFORE
A GANGSTA SAVED XMAS
IN A HUSTLER I TRUST
By **Monet Dragun**

TIPPIN THE SCALES 2 | DIESEL

QUIET MONEY 1-3
THUG LIFE 1-3
EXTENDED CLIP 1&2
A GANGSTA'S PARADISE
By **Trai'Quan**

CAUGHT UP IN THE LIFE 1-3
THE STREETS NEVER LET GO 1-3
By **Robert Baptiste**

NEW TO THE GAME 1-3
MONEY, MURDER & MEMORIES 1-3
By **Malik D. Rice**

THE LIFE OF A HOOD STAR
By **Ca$h & Rashia Wilson**

THE STREETS WILL NEVER CLOSE 1-4
By **K'ajji**

LIFE OF A SAVAGE 1-4
A GANGSTA'S QUR'AN 1-4
MURDA SEASON 1-3
GANGLAND CARTEL 1-3
CHI'RAQ GANGSTAS 1-4
KILLERS ON ELM STREET 1-3
JACK BOYZ N DA BRONX 1-3
A DOPEBOY'S DREAM 1-3
JACK BOYS VS DOPE BOYS 1-3
COKE GIRLZ
COKE BOYS
SOSA GANG 1&2
BRONX SAVAGES
BODYMORE KINGPINS
BLOOD OF A GOON
By **Romell Tukes**

TIPPIN THE SCALES 2 | DIESEL

CREAM 2-3
THE STREETS WILL TALK
By **Yolanda Moore**

CONCRETE KILLA 1-3
VICIOUS LOYALTY 1-3
By **Kingpen**

THE ULTIMATE SACRIFICE 1-6
KHADIFI
IF YOU CROSS ME ONCE 1-5
ANGEL 1-4
IN THE BLINK OF AN EYE
By **Anthony Fields**

NIGHTMARES OF A HUSTLA 1-3
BLOOD AND GAMES 1&2
By **King Dream**

HARD AND RUTHLESS 1&2
MOB TOWN 251
THE BILLIONAIRE BENTLEYS 1-3
REAL G'S MOVE IN SILENCE
By **Von Diesel**

MOB TIES 1-7
SOUL OF A HUSTLER, HEART OF A KILLER 1-3
GORILLAZ IN THE TRENCHES
By **SayNoMore**

BODYMORE MURDERLAND 1-3
THE BIRTH OF A GANGSTER 1-4
By **Delmont Player**

FOR THE LOVE OF A BOSS 1&2
By **C. D. Blue**

KILLA KOUNTY 1-5
By **Khufu**

MOBBED UP 1-4
THE BRICK MAN 1-5
THE COCAINE PRINCESS 1-10
STEPPERS 1-3
SUPER GREMLIN 1-4
By **King Rio**

MONEY GAME 1&2
By **Smoove Dolla**

A GANGSTA'S KARMA 1-4
By **FLAME**

KING OF THE TRENCHES 1-3
By **GHOST & TRANAY ADAMS**

QUEEN OF THE ZOO 1&2
By **Black Migo**

GRIMEY WAYS 1-3
BETRAYAL OF A G
By **Ray Vinci**

XMAS WITH AN ATL SHOOTER
By **Ca$h & Destiny Skai**

KING KILLA 1&2
By **Vincent "Vitto" Holloway**

BETRAYAL OF A THUG 1&2
By **Fre$h**

TIPPIN THE SCALES 2 | DIESEL

THE MURDER QUEENS 1-6
By **Michael Gallon**

FOR THE LOVE OF BLOOD 1-4
By **Jamel Mitchell**

HOOD CONSIGLIERE 1&2
NO TIME FOR ERROR
By **Keese**

PROTÉGÉ OF A LEGEND 1&2
LOVE IN THE TRENCHES 1&2
By **Corey Robinson**

THE PLUG'S RUTHLESS DAUGHTER 1&2
By **Tony Daniels**

BORN IN THE GRAVE 1-3
CRIME PAYS 1&2
By **Self Made Tay**

MOAN IN MY MOUTH
By **XTASY**

TORN BETWEEN A GANGSTER AND A
GENTLEMAN
By **J-BLUNT & Miss Kim**

HERE TODAY GONE TOMORROW 1&2
By **Fly Rock**

PILLOW PRINCESS
By **S. Hawkins**

SANCTIFIED AND HORNY
by **XTASY**

WOMEN LIE MEN LIE 1-4
FIFTY SHADES OF SNOW 1-3
STACK BEFORE YOU SPLURGE
GIRLS FALL LIKE DOMINOES
NAÏVE TO THE STREETS
By **ROY MILLIGAN**

LOYALTY IS EVERYTHING 1-3
CITY OF SMOKE 1&2
By **Molotti**

THE BUTTERFLY MAFIA 1-4
SALUTE MY SAVAGERY 1&2
By **Fumiya Payne**

THE LANE 1&2
By **Ken-Ken Spence**

THE PUSSY TRAP 1-5
By **Nene Capri**

DIRTY DNA
By **Blaque**

BOOKS BY LDP'S CEO, CA$H

TRUST IN NO MAN
TRUST IN NO MAN 2
TRUST IN NO MAN 3
BONDED BY BLOOD
SHORTY GOT A THUG
THUGS CRY
THUGS CRY 2
THUGS CRY 3
TRUST NO BITCH
TRUST NO BITCH 2
TRUST NO BITCH 3
TIL MY CASKET DROPS
RESTRAINING ORDER
RESTRAINING ORDER 2
IN LOVE WITH A CONVICT
LIFE OF A HOOD STAR
XMAS WITH AN ATL SHOOTER

www.ingramcontent.com/pod-product-compliance
Lightning Source LLC
Chambersburg PA
CBHW071152260626
47162CB00003B/1022